KW

Dear Reader,

Okay, I confess, I'm fascinated with twins. I sometimes try to imagine my life as it would be if I had a twin. When I was a child, I always wanted to be one of a set of twins. The most fun would be switching places and fooling people—so I thought.

Alas, I am not a twin, nor do twins run in my family. But the fascination remains. This story is about twins—sheikhs no less. The fact that they are twins does not play a huge role in the linked stories, but there is that mystique. Do twins think alike? Not always. Otherwise each twin would want to marry the same person.

Sometimes, despite looking identical, their interests are vastly different and the lives they lead as individual as anyone's. In this story the older twin, by seven minutes, leads a life of high-stakes oil and international business dealings. He loves the challenge of dealing in the world market. Just when he's about to sign a strategic contract, things get dicey and he needs help from an unlikely source.

Can two very different lifestyles be blended? Of course—if you have love. Please join me on this fun journey as Rashid and Bethanne discover the greatest gift of all.

Two brothers, twins to boot, find love and happy futures in totally unexpected ways.

All the best,

Barbara

BARBARA McMAHON

Accidentally the Sheikh's Wife

JEWELS of the DESERT

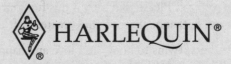

HARLEQUIN®

TORONTO • NEW YORK • LONDON
AMSTERDAM • PARIS • SYDNEY • HAMBURG
STOCKHOLM • ATHENS • TOKYO • MILAN • MADRID
PRAGUE • WARSAW • BUDAPEST • AUCKLAND

Recycling programs
for this product may
not exist in your area.

ISBN-13: 978-0-373-17644-1

ACCIDENTALLY THE SHEIKH'S WIFE

First North American Publication 2010.

Copyright © 2010 by Barbara McMahon.

www.eHarlequin.com

Printed in U.S.A.

Barbara McMahon was born and raised in the U.S. South, but settled in California after spending a year flying around the world for an international airline. After settling down to raise a family and work for a computer firm, she began writing when her children started school. Now, feeling fortunate in being able to realize the long-held dream of quitting her day job and writing full-time, she and her husband have moved to the Sierra Nevada of California, where she finds her desire to write is stronger than ever. With the beauty of the mountains visible from her windows, and the pace of life slower than that of the hectic San Francisco Bay Area, where they previously resided, she finds more time than ever to think up stories and characters and share them with others through writing. Barbara loves to hear from readers. You can reach her at P.O. Box 977, Pioneer, CA 95666-0977, U.S.A. Readers can also contact Barbara at her Web site, www.barbaramcmahon.com.

To Carol, Barbara, Kate, Diana, Lynn and Candice.
Thanks a bunch.
Lunch is always great fun.

CHAPTER ONE

BETHANNE SANDERS lined up the aircraft with the designated runway and began the final descent. The new jet handled like a dream—all the way from Texas to the coast of the Persian Gulf. It was the first time she'd flown halfway around the world and she wished she could continue on until she circled the globe. When she left Quishari, it would be by commercial flight back through Europe.

Maybe she'd get another dream assignment like this one in the not-too-distant future. For now, she continued to scan the landscape as far as she could see as the plane began descending. Excitement built. The Persian Gulf was magnificently blue, from deep, dark navy to shades of azure and turquoise. The strip of sandy beach now visible was almost blinding beneath the sun. She had read so much about Quishari and heard so much from her father, she almost felt like she recognized the landmarks as she came in for the landing. Her heart raced at the thought of actually being here. It was like a dream come true.

Had this assignment not materialized, she still would have come—but it might have taken longer as the cost was exorbitant and savings accumulated slowly.

But fate had stepped in—almost like the answer to a

prayer. She was delivering a brand-new Starcraft jet to Sheikh Rashid al Harum—and bringing in a priceless cargo. His soon-to-be fiancée.

Except for the shakedown trips around Texas, the only hours on this jet were the ones taken to fly it here. If the sheikh liked it and accepted delivery, he'd be the proud owner of the latest and greatest of the Starcraft line.

She hoped the sheikh's fiancée enjoyed the detailing of the luxury appointments and had enjoyed the flight. Bethanne had taken extra care to make the journey as smooth as possible. She found it vastly romantic that they were planning to marry—and neither had yet met the other.

A bit odd in the twenty-first century. Still, to have been chosen to be the bride of one of the fabulously wealthy sheikhs of Quishari had to be thrilling. Pictures had been exchanged, the parents had made the arrangements. How did a thirty-four-year-old man feel about having his bride handpicked? Not too different from some of the online dating services—match likes and dislikes, find someone compatible, and there they were.

Would they kiss when meeting? Seal the deal, so to speak? Or would the woman be too shy to be bold enough for physical affection at the instant of meeting?

She had daydreamed on the long portions of the flight when autopilot had taken care of flying that she was being met by someone who would sweep her off her feet, make her feel cherished and special.

Or, alternatively, she'd also imagined her father striding along the tarmac, gathering her into his arms for one of his big bear hugs.

Blinking, Bethanne brought her attention back to the task of landing this multimillion-dollar jet.

The snowy-white exterior had already been detailed with

stripes using the colors of Quishari—blue and gold and green. The interior resembled a high-end hotel lobby. The lush Persian carpet in golds and reds supported cushy sofas and armchairs, all with the requisite seat belts. The small dining area was elegant with rich walnut furnishings. The galley was fully stocked, and included a stove, oven and microwave in addition to the lavish below-counter refrigerator, wider than long, capable of carrying any supplies necessary for the sheikh's pleasure. Even the sole restroom was spacious.

Bethanne had shown Haile al Benqura all the features of the cabin before going to the cockpit for her preflight routine. The chaperone accompanying the young woman had not spoken English, but Haile had. She'd taken in everything with a solemn demeanor. Wasn't she the slightest bit excited? Apparently when the sheikh had mentioned something to the president of Starcraft, her boss had immediately offered to fly Haile from her home in Morocco to Quishari as a favor to the prospective buyer of their top-of-the-line private jet.

Bethanne glanced at her copilot, Jess Bradshaw. It was his first long-distance delivery as well and they had taken turns flying the aircraft to minimize delivery time.

"Want to bring it in?" she asked.

"No. We want this to go perfectly. I'm not as good at it as you."

She shrugged and then brought the plane down with a kiss against the asphalt.

"Nice job," Jess said.

"Thanks. This is a sweetheart of a plane. The sheikh is one lucky man."

She followed directions from the tower and taxied to an area away from the main terminal. The immaculate hangar was already swarming with ground crew; everyone had eyes on the jet as she pulled it into the designated slot. She and Jess ran through the checklist as they shut down. She wanted to

dash out and breathe the Quishari air. But duty first. She had
scheduled several days here to see if she could find her dad.
And to see the towns and desert that made Quishari famous.

"I'm glad we get to sleep on the way home," Jess
mumbled, waiting for her to get up first. He followed her
from the cockpit to the outside door of the jet. With
minimum effort, Bethanne opened it, watching as stairs
unfolded. She glanced back and saw the chaperone. Where
was Haile? In the restroom? Probably primping to look her
best when seeing the sheikh for the first time. Bethanne
hoped she hadn't been there when they landed. Jess had an-
nounced their approach and told the passengers to fasten
seat belts.

The chaperone looked worried, her eyes darting around the
cabin, refusing to meet Bethanne's gaze. Had she been afraid
of flying? Bethanne couldn't image anyone not loving it.
She'd wanted to be a pilot since she turned five and first been
taken up in the cockpit of a small plane. Of course, wanting
to follow in her father's footsteps had also played a big part.

Two men waited at the foot of the stairs. When the steps
unfolded and locked in place, the taller began to ascend.
Bethanne watched him approach. He was maybe six-three or
four. Which Bethanne found refreshing. Her own five-ten
height usually had her eye to eye with men. His dark hair
shone in the sunlight, his skin was tanned to teak. The closer
he came, the more she could see—from dark eyes that watched
her steadily, to a strong jaw that suggested arrogance and
power, to the wide shoulders encased in a pristine white shirt
and dark charcoal suit.

Her heart began to beat heavily. She was fascinated by the
man. Awareness flooded through her, as did a sudden need to
brush her hair—she hoped it was still neat in its French plait.
Studying him as he drew closer every step, she noticed the hint

of wave in his hair. She wondered what he'd look like if he ran his fingers through his hair. Or if she did.

She swallowed and tried to look away. Fantasies like that would get her nowhere. This had to be Sheikh Rashid al Harum. Almost-fiancé to the woman in the back of the plane. Oh, lucky Haile al Benqura. She had undoubtedly fallen in love with the man from the pictures exchanged. Now she would be greeted and swept off her feet with one of the most gorgeous men Bethanne had ever seen.

"I am Rashid al Harum. Welcome to Quishari," he said in English as he stepped into the aircraft.

"Thank you." She cleared her throat. That husky tone wasn't like her. This man was rattling her senses. "I'm Bethanne Sanders. My copilot, Jess Bradshaw." She saw the surprise in his eyes. Despite all the headway women had made in aviation, it was still considered primarily a male profession. She was growing used to seeing that expression—especially in locales away from the U.S.

Rashid al Harum inclined his head slightly and then looked beyond them into the cabin.

The older woman rose and began to speak in a rapid strained tone.

Bethanne still didn't see Haile. Was she ill? As the chaperone continued, she glanced at the sheikh, wishing she understood the language. His face grew harder by the second. In a moment he turned and glared at Bethanne. "What do you know of Haile's disappearance?" he asked in English.

Bethanne looked back into the cabin. "Disappearance? Isn't she in the restroom?" she asked, suddenly worried something was wrong. What had the chaperone said? Where was Haile al Benqura?

"Apparently she never left Morocco," the sheikh said in a tight voice.

"What? That's impossible. I showed her around the plane myself. She was on board when we were ready to leave." She turned to Jess. "You saw her, right? When you boarded?"

Jess shook his head slightly. "I don't remember seeing her when I closed the door. A maintenance man ran down the stairs just as I was rounding the back to board. No one else got off the plane."

"There shouldn't have been a maintenance man aboard—there's nothing wrong with the plane," Bethanne said. What was going on? Where was Haile? "What did she say?" Bethanne gestured to the chaperone, still standing in front of the sofa.

The sheikh glared at her for a moment, then in a soft, controlled voice that did not soothe at all, said, "I suggest that you and I speak alone."

She stared at him, suddenly worried things had gone terribly wrong. He seemed to tower above her, anger evident.

"I'll check on things on the ground," Jess said with obvious relief. He eased by the two of them and hurried down the stairs. Once he was out of earshot, the sheikh turned to the older woman and spoke briefly.

She dropped her gaze and nodded. Gathering her few things, she walked to the back and sat on the edge of the sofa, gazing out one of the small windows.

"According to her, Haile took off before the plane departed Morocco, running to meet a lover."

"What? How is that possible? I thought she was coming here to meet you—your fiancée, or almost," Bethanne blurted out before thinking. How could the woman choose someone else over this man? was Bethanne's first thought.

"So she is, was, to be. Her family and mine have been in negotiations for months over an oil deal that would prove advantageous to both countries. Included in that was the merger of our two families through marriage. Now my entire family—

not to mention others in this country—expects the arrival of a woman who is to be my wife—and she is not on board."

Bethanne swallowed hard at the anger in his eyes. Surreptitiously wiping her palms against the fabric of her uniform, she raised her chin and said, "I'm not responsible for her leaving the plane. I thought she was on board. She was when I last saw her."

"You're the captain of the aircraft. What goes on is your responsibility. I hold you accountable. How could you let her leave?" His dark eyes pinned her in place. His entire demeanor shimmered with anger—controlled, which made it seem even stronger.

"How was I suppose to know she didn't want to come here? I thought everything was arranged." She would not tell him how romantic she found the scenario. Maybe she hadn't thought it through if the woman had fled rather than come to Quishari. "Though if I had known the circumstances, maybe I would have questioned whether anyone wanted to be *negotiated* into a marriage. I thought it was an old-fashioned mail-order-bride situation. But if the bride wasn't willing, I'm glad I did not have a part in bringing her here." She looked at the older woman. "She's the one you should hold responsible. Bringing them from Morocco to Quishari was a favor to you by our company."

"But the favor was not fulfilled. She is not here."

"I can see that. What do you want me to do about it now?" Bethanne said.

"The marriage would be an arrangement that benefits both countries," he said with a dismissing gesture. "That is not any concern of yours. The decision has been made. What is of your concern, is the fact Haile went missing on your watch."

Bethanne met his gaze bravely. It was not her fault the woman had deplaned. Why hadn't the chaperone stopped her? Or told someone before they took off from Morocco? What else could she say?

This was certainly not the happy arrival at Quishari she'd anticipated.

"The immediate need, now, is for damage control," he said after a moment. The sheikh looked back at the woman sitting so still in the back of the jet. For a moment Bethanne imagined she could see the wheels spinning in his head. How could she have known Haile wasn't as interested in the marriage as she had thought? She would never have suspected a young woman like Haile would disguise herself and slip away between the time Bethanne went into the cockpit and Jess joined her. It couldn't have been more than five minutes. Obviously it had not been a spur-of-the-moment decision. It had taken planning and daring. Bethanne's romantic mind imagined Haile deplaning surreptitiously and finding her lover and both fleeing, whilst her father and his minions followed on horseback. She blinked. Her overactive imagination could get her in trouble.

"I'm sorry I can't help you," she said, hoping to ease the tension that was as thick as butter. Her primary goal was to deliver the plane, which she'd done. Now all the sheikh had to do was accept the delivery, sign the paperwork and Bethanne could begin her vacation in Quishari while Jess would be flying back to Texas on the next available flight.

"Ah, but you can help. In fact, I insist." He turned back to her. The serious expression in his eyes held her in thrall. What did he mean?

"How can I help? Fly back to Morocco and find her? I wouldn't begin to know where to look."

"Despite my family's efforts to keep the entire matter solely within the family, rumors have been flying around the country. I've ignored them, but I know they speculate a special visitor will arrive soon. My coming to meet this plane would have fueled speculation even more. So, you're it."

"I'm what it?" she asked, wondering what would happen if there was no special visitor. Some gossip, more speculation about when his fiancée would arrive.

"The woman I came to meet. It's as if it was meant to be. What are the odds of having a female pilot bringing the plane—and one who is young and pretty enough to pass muster?"

"Muster for what?" Bethanne wondered if she'd fallen down the rabbit hole. Nothing was making sense.

"To pass as my special guest, of course."

She stared at him. "Are you crazy? I mean…" Ever conscious of the fact he was an important client of her company she didn't want to insult, she stopped. But he couldn't be serious. Thinking she could pass as a fiancée for a sheikh? He had to have half the money of the country. She'd learned that much about the al Harum family from her father. They controlled vast oil deposits and dealt in the world market for oil. They played a major role in the government of Quishari and had for generations.

Bethanne's head was spinning. He wanted to pretend she was his fiancée?

He spoke to the chaperone who came reluctantly to stand beside him. For several moments, he spoke in rapid Arabic. The woman glanced at Bethanne and frowned. The sheikh continued to speak and resignation settled on the woman's face. Finally she answered, bowing slightly.

Bethanne hadn't understood a word. But her mind had quickly considered and discarded one idea after another. The one fact that shone above all was she would be dealing with Rashid al Harum for days. Awareness spiked. She wished she had checked her makeup and hair before opening the door. Did he even see her in the uniform? Feeling decidedly feminine to his masculinity, she let herself consider the out-landish suggestion.

Special guest to a sheikh. They'd spend a lot of romantic moments together. Would he kiss her? Her knees almost melted at the thought.

"It is settled. Haile's chaperone will serve as yours for the time being. Her name is Fatima. She doesn't speak English but we'll get around that somehow."

"Wait a minute. I'm not—"

He raised his hand. "You are in my country now, Ms. Sanders. And my rules apply. Certain influential people are watching to see the young woman that I am interested in. It is fortunate that my family kept a tight lid on the negotiations. No one knows who I have selected. It would not be a good thing at this point to disappoint them. You are my choice since *you* lost my other one."

"That's totally ridiculous. How can you say that? Maybe you need a few minutes to come up with an alternative plan."

"This suits me. Time is short. Please put on a happy face and accompany me down the stairs," he ordered.

"Wait a minute. I haven't agreed to anything."

"Would you prefer to fly this plane back to the United States immediately? Canceling the sale?" he asked. "And perhaps putting in jeopardy the relationship Quishari holds with Morocco?"

His implacable expression confirmed he was completely serious. She tried to comprehend if he really thought she could divert an international incident. She opened her mouth to refute it when a thought occurred to her.

She had another agenda in Quishari. She had hoped during her vacation to find her father. It wasn't exactly the kind of stay she'd envisioned, but maybe agreeing to his pretense for a short time would work to her advantage as well. Certainly the special guest of the sheikh would be afforded more access to information than a mere visitor. She had contacts to find, places to visit. Wouldn't it be easier with the help of Sheikh Rashid al Harum?

She closed her mouth while she tried to see how this odd request—no, demand—could work to her benefit. "What exactly are we talking about?" she asked, suddenly seeing the situation advantageous to her own quest.

"A short visit. We'll tell people you've come to meet me and my family. If they think you and I are making a match, that's their problem. After a few weeks, you leave. By then, I'll have the contract finalized and who cares what the rumormongers say. In the meantime, you would be my honored guest."

"I don't see how that would work at all. We don't even know each other." She had never been in love. Had dreamed about finding that special man, one who had likes and interests similar to her own. Never in a million years could she envision herself having anything in common with a sheikh. But there was that pull of attraction that surprised her. She couldn't fall for a stranger. Not right away. It had to be jet lag or something.

Still, he fascinated her. And she was pragmatic enough to realize she could get a lot of help in searching for her father.

The way he put things, it wasn't quite as if they were supposed to be lovers. They were to be still in the getting-to-know-you stage. The thought of getting to know him better tantalized. And people who were almost engaged did kiss.

Why did that compel her? she wondered as she looked at his lips, imagining them pressed against her own.

"Have you considered all the ramifications? What will you say when asked how we met? Why we are attracted to each other? My background is not that important that a sheikh would view it as any kind of advantage."

"Perhaps we could say we fell in love," he suggested sardonically.

She frowned. His tone suggested he didn't believe in love. The dismissing glance he gave proved the thought never crossed his mind. And it wasn't as if she'd fallen in love with him. A strong interest in an intriguing man—that's all she felt. Once she got to know him better, she'd undoubtedly find him a bit annoying.

"It's important even in an arranged marriage for the partners to at least be cordial to each other," she replied with false sweetness, wondering if she could spend much time in his company without coming completely unglued.

"Do you not think I can be cordial?" he asked in a silky tone, leaning closer. He brushed his fingers against her cheek as he pushed back a strand of hair. His dark eyes were so close she could see tiny golden flecks in them. The affinity she felt was drugging. She wanted to close the scant inches separating them and touch his face, feel his mouth on hers.

She drew a breath to get control of her senses. But the scent of his aftershave set her senses to dancing. She opened her mouth to offer a hearty no, then closed it.

Think.

It would help her look for her father. Using her unexpected position to gain access where mere visitors might not have was a bonus she never expected. Don't hastily reject this, she warned herself.

"Perhaps," she conceded.

"And you?" he asked. The intensity of his gaze had her mesmerized. She could no more look away than she could fly without a plane.

"I can be cordial. But not lovey-dovey," she said. There was a limit she dare not cross lest she be lost. One kiss would never be enough. She'd become demanding and forget why she'd come to Quishari if the tempting allure was given free rein.

Amusement flared in his eyes. "Agreed, no lovey-dovey. You must call me Rashid and I will call you Bethanne. In public you will appear to be devoted to me."

"And in private?" she asked, already wondering if she'd lost her mind to even consider such a bizarre plan. Still, if it gave her the answers she craved, who was she to say no?

"I'd settle for devotion, but can understand if you feel more reserved," he said. Laughter lurked in his eyes.

The amusement confused her. Was he serious or not?

"I will have Fatima accompany you to a villa I own by the sea. It was where Haile was to stay. You'll have privacy there. Of course, I expect you to attend the celebratory functions that have been planned. And to convince my mother we have a chance of making this work."

"Your mother? You want to pretend to your mother? I think you're crazy."

Bethanne was not close to her own mother but lying to her would never be an option. Were the sheikh and his mother on no better terms?

The amusement vanished. "I want nothing to ruin the deal I still have pending with Haile's father. There are factions here who oppose the proposed arrangement. The finance minister, for one. He would consider Haile's actions an insult to our country. He'd love nothing better than to drive a wedge into the negotiations. As it stands, perhaps it is even better that things turned out this way. Al Benqura will feel guilty at the actions of his daughter so be more willing to concede some points still to be agreed upon. Help me and I will do something in return for you."

Mixed feelings washed through her. She could never pull off being a woman of interest to a dynamic man like Rashid al Harum. She'd be spotted for a fraud the first time she ventured out. Yet the thought of being escorted around by him had her stomach flipping over in giddy anticipation. She'd never have this kind of chance again.

She had only seconds to make a decision.

Jess stepped to the door. "Everything okay?" he asked.

Rashid did not look away from Bethanne. Her gaze met his, seeking assurance that if she complied with this wild scheme, it would end up all right for all.

"Everything is fine," she said at last, hoping she wasn't making a monumental mistake.

There was an almost imperceptible change in the sheikh's manner. Had he doubted her? Well, he should. If not for her goal of finding her father, she would have categorically denied his request. Or maybe thought about it a bit longer. She had trouble looking away.

The sheikh spun around. "There is no need for you to remain. We can get you on a plane within the hour to return to the United States." The sheikh summoned the other man still standing at the foot of the stairs. In only seconds, Sheikh Rashid al Harum had given him orders.

One less person who would know about the charade, Bethanne thought. She was still a bit bemused with the entire matter. This man knew what he wanted and went for it without hesitation.

"Bethanne?" Jess said, looking between her and the sheikh as if suspecting something was amiss.

"I'll be fine. Just a few details to work out. If you can get on a plane within the hour, you better take advantage of the flight."

"In the meantime, I will examine the interior and cockpit," Rashid said.

Jess came closer to Bethanne when Rashid went to inspect the rear of the plane. "Is everything really okay? What happened to the fiancée?" he whispered.

"Um, change of plans."

Jess still appeared doubtful, but he nodded and turned to retrieve his bag from where he'd stashed it. With one more look down the cabin, he turned and left with the sheikh's man.

The sheikh peered out of one of the side windows and watched as Jess entered the car that had been waiting and was soon heading for the main section of the busy airport.

He nodded as if in satisfaction and headed for the front of the plane.

"I assume you have your own bags," he said.

She nodded and pointed out the small travel case she used.

"You travel light."

"It carries enough clothes for me. Two more uniforms like the one I'm wearing. And some off-duty outfits. I have reservations at a hotel in the heart of the city," she said.

"You were planning to stay in Quishari for a while?"

"Yes. I've heard about it for years. Have pictures and books and pamphlets about the beaches, the history and the stark desert dwellings. I'm quite looking forward to learning more firsthand. I think I'm already in love with the country."

"Where did you learn this?" he asked.

"From my father, Hank Pendarvis."

For a moment she wondered at the change in attitude of the sheikh. His face tightened as it had when he learned of Haile's defection.

"Your name is Sanders," he said.

"My stepfather's name. My mother remarried when I was young and he adopted me. We do not get along. My father has been missing for three years."

"He is a thief. He stole one of our planes."

She blinked. "That's a lie!" Her father was not a thief.

"So you are the daughter of a thief." Rashid shook his head.

"No, I'm not. That's not true. My father would never steal

anything—especially from your family. He wrote how he loved working for Bashiri Oil and for Sheikh Rabid al Harum."

"My father. Who died when he learned of Hank's theft."

Bethanne felt sick. Was it possible? No, not her father. She hadn't seen much of him over the years, but she had scads of letters. And he'd phoned her once a week for most of her life. Whenever he was in the States, he came to visit. They flew over Texas, had picnics in meadows and spent time at the beach together. She loved those visits when her father would tell her of the ideal life he enjoyed flying for the senior al Harum.

She raised her chin. "You are wrong."

Rashid uttered a word in Arabic she did not understand. But the intent was clear. He did not like this situation at all. Did he want to change the role she was to play?

He leaned forward, anger radiating from him. "My family has been hurt by yours already. Do not betray me in this charade or it will be the worst for you. I am stuck—temporarily—but do not think I shall forget for an instant."

"If you want my help, you need to make good your offer to do something for me in return."

"And that is?" he asked, his demeanor suddenly suspicious.

"Help me find my father."

He stared at her for a long moment, then stepped to the door. He gestured to someone on the ground and the man entered a moment later. He lifted Bethanne's carry-on bag and went back.

"Agreed. But if we find him, the law will take care of him."

"Not if he didn't steal a plane," she countered. She wasn't sure if she was relieved or stressed at the thought of being the sheikh's girlfriend. But if it helped her to find her father, she would make the best of it.

"So we begin," the sheikh said and stepped to the top step.

Bethanne followed, Fatima behind her. There were now several men in suits at the bottom of the stairs and they came to attention as the sheikh appeared. Bethanne felt caught in a dream. She glided down the stairs and before she knew it, she was in the back of a stretch limousine that seemed to take up a city block. It was a luxurious machine, gleaming white beneath the hot sun, with fancy gold Arabic script on the doors. When she stepped inside, Bethanne was delighted with the cold air that greeted her. Fatima rode in front beside the driver. Rashid slid onto the wide backseat with her. A few words and the driver had the glass wall slide up, separating them from the front of the vehicle.

She glanced at the sheikh as they drove away. He flipped on a cell phone and was speaking rapidly, the Arabic words beyond her. He didn't look like he was taking all the air in the car, but she felt breathless. Gazing out the window, she tried to quell her riotous emotions. She could reach out and touch him—had she the right? Clenching her hands into fists, she refused to give way to the clamoring attention his presence demanded. He thought her father was a thief. How dare he! She had best remember this was only a game of pretense while he went after that oil deal. For her part, he agreed to help her find her father. It would be worth it in the end as long as she kept her head.

Fruitless daydreams of a relationship between them would contribute nothing. She had to keep focused and ignore the awareness that seemed to grow the longer she was around him.

Hank Pendarvis had disappeared three years ago. She feared he was dead. Her mother, long ago divorced and re-married, had tried to obtain information from the oil company for which he flew—the one owned by the sheikh—but her inquiries had produced no results. Bethanne had tried letters to people her father had mentioned over the years, but only one had gone through and that person had not known anything beyond Hank had flown away one day and never returned.

Bethanne missed the larger-than-life man, her secret hero from childhood. He'd been the one to spark her interest in flying, her passion for exploring new places, meeting new people. He would not have ignored her this long if he were alive.

Sad as it was to think of him as dead, she wanted closure. To know what happened to him. And if he were dead, where he lay. She tried to convince herself he was dead or would have contacted her. But the faint hope he was just caught up in something could not be quenched. Until she knew, she hoped he was still alive somewhere.

"We are here," Rashid said.

Bethanne blinked and turned her head to peer out his window as the car slowed and turned into the wide driveway that led to a beautiful white villa. A stunning expanse of green grass blanketed the area in front of the structure. It looked like an Italian home or French Riviera villa. Nothing like what she expected in an Arabic country.

"Wow," she murmured softly. The home was amazing. Two stories tall with a wraparound veranda on both levels, its white walls gleamed in the sunshine. The red terra cotta roof sloped down, providing cover to the upper veranda which in turn shaded the lower level. Tall French doors opened from every room.

The driveway curved around in front, flanked by banks of blue and gold flowers. The chauffeur slowed to a stop in front of wide double doors, with wooden panels carved in ornate designs. The heavy wrought-iron handles added substance. The right door opened even before the car stopped. A tall man wearing traditional robes stepped outside and hastened down the shallow steps to open the passenger door.

The sheikh stepped out and returned the man's greetings.

"Mohammad, this is Ms. Sanders. She has come to stay for a while as my special guest," he said in English.

Less than five minutes later Bethanne stood alone in the large bedroom that had been assigned to her. It held a huge canopy bed in the center, complete with steps to the high mattress. The chandelier in the center of the ceiling sparkled in the light streaming in through the open French doors. Gauzy curtains gently swayed in the light breeze.

Two sets of French doors gave access to the wide upper veranda. She stepped outside and immediately inhaled the tang of the sea mixed with the fragrance of hundreds of flowers blossoming beneath her. She crossed to the railing and gazed at the profusion of colors and shapes in the garden below. A wide path led from the garden toward the sea, a glimpse of which she could see from where she stood. Walking along the veranda toward the Gulf, she was enchanted to find a better vantage point at the corner with a clear view to a sugar-white beach and the lovely blue water.

The maid who had shown her to her room had thankfully spoken English. She told Bethanne her name was Minnah while she unpacked the few articles of clothing in the small bag and asked if Bethanne had more luggage coming.

At a loss, she merely shook her head and continued staring at the garden.

She'd have to suggest to the sheikh that a woman coming to visit would bring more than a handful of uniforms and an assortment of casual clothes. This stupid plan of his would never work. What did he hope to achieve? Save the embarrassment of people learning his intended bride had run away rather than go through with a marriage? Get the business deal completed without anyone knowing how insulting Haile al Benqura's actions had been?

She had no idea of how long he expected this charade to last. So any investigations for her father needed to be done swiftly in case her visit was cut radically short. The sheikh had canceled her reservations at the hotel. She wondered if she should make new ones, just in case.

After she'd changed and freshened up, Bethanne headed back down the way she'd come. The villa wasn't as large as she first thought. Probably only eight bedroom suites. She almost laughed at the thought. Her tiny apartment in Galveston would squeeze into her assigned bedroom here.

She didn't see a soul as she went back to the front door and let herself out. The limo was gone. The lawn stretched out to a tall flowering hedge of oleander, sheltering the house from any view from the street.

Following the lower veranda to the path she'd seen, Bethanne walked through the garden and out to the beach. There were several chairs and tables on the white sand near the edge of the garden. She could sit and relax after her walk.

In the distance she saw a large container ship slowly moving through the Gulf. Happily Bethanne walked to the water's edge, kicked off her shoes and started walking north. Her mind was already formulating where she could begin with her inquiries. When she returned to the villa, she'd summons the maid to begin with her. Had her father ever visited the house? Maybe the staff would remember him. She wanted answers and didn't plan to leave Quishari until she had them. Neither the difficulty of the task nor language barrier would stop her!

"What's got you upset?" Khalid asked from his position lounging on one of the chairs in Rashid's office at Bashiri Oil. The corner office had a splendid view of Alkaahdar and the Gulf. On the highest floor of the building, it rose above most other buildings in the capital city and gave an unimpeded view.

Rashid paced to the tall window and glared at the cityscape, annoyed afresh that his brother had picked up on his irritation. It was not new. Twins had an uncanny intuition concerning each other. Rashid could recognize his brother's moods in a second. Of course Khalid could recognize his.

He knew he had to contact Haile's father. The longer he delayed, the more awkward it would become. Did the man know yet his daughter had run off? Had he known about the other man all along and still expected Haile to consider marriage to him?

He turned from the window and met his brother's eyes. Khalid had the knack of instant relaxation. And then instant action when called for. He was slouched on one of the visitor chairs. Rashid noted his brother was wearing a suit again, instead of the more traditional robes. A concession to being in the city. First chance he had, Rashid knew his brother would head for the interior or the derricks along the coast to the south. Khalid was not one for society or social niceties.

For a second he debated trying the charade on his twin. But it would not take long for Khalid to figure things out. Besides, they had never lied to each other.

"It appears the glowing bride-to-be is glowing for someone else."

"Huh?" Khalid sat up at that. "What do you mean?"

"She never arrived."

"I heard she did and that she's blonde and tall and you whisked her away to keep her from the prying eyes of everyone."

"The rumor mill is even faster than I knew. That's the idea. Haile never arrived. I want to finalize the deal with al Benqura before letting the world know I've been stood up. You know what the minister would say if he found out. This deal's too important to me to let some flighty woman screw it up." Briefly Rashid outlined the situation.

"What does al Benqura say to his daughter's no-show?" Khalid asked.

"I'm not sure he knows."

"And the blonde you escorted from the plane?"

"I hope a substitute until the deal is done."

"Where did you conjure her up?"

"Turns out she's the pilot delivering my new plane—that was supposed to bring Haile. She thought Haile was on board and was as surprised as I was to discover she was not."

"Ah, yes, the new jet you're buying. The pilot is a woman? That's odd."

"Or providence in this situation."

"And she agreed to this charade? What am I saying, of course she did. How much for her silence?"

Rashid shrugged. "So far no monetary demands. But a twist I never expected. She's Hank Pendarvis's daughter."

"What?" Khalid sat up at that. "You're kidding. I didn't even know he had a family."

"And she's looking for her father."

Khalid sat up in his chair. "He took that jet some years ago."

"And disappeared. Apparently starting life anew, he cut all ties with his past. She wants to know what happened. As do we all."

Khalid shrugged. "Don't get in too deep," he warned. "I wouldn't trust her, if I were you." He shifted slightly and tilted his head in a manner that reminded Rashid of his own mannerisms when confronted by questionable behavior. "Are you sure she won't give away the scheme at the first chance? European tabloids would love such a story. And she has nothing to lose and lots of money to gain."

"So far she seems more interested in searching for her father than acquiring anything. But I will keep in mind her relationship to Hank."

Rashid glanced back out the window, but he knew he wasn't fooling his twin. That Bethanne would refuse to cooperate was a true risk. One he was willing to take to insure the finalization of the deal he had been working on for months.

He needed the support of the ministry to finalize the deal of such magnitude. Otherwise he wouldn't care two figs about the minister's position.

He was not going to tell his brother how he had grown to regret agreeing to an engagement that had been so strongly encouraged between his mother and al Benqura. Haile had the perfect background to be his wife. And after his aborted attempt to marry the woman of his choice when he was twenty-two, Haile seemed more than suitable.

He also was not going to mention the flash of desire that had surprised him when he met Bethanne. She was so different from the women he knew. If asked for a type, he would have said he preferred petite and dark, with brown eyes and a lush figure. Bethanne didn't meet a single criterion. She was tall, blonde, blue eyes and almost as slender as a boy.

But that didn't stop his interest. Which hadn't waned even when learning she was Hank's daughter. There could be nothing between them. Not once the relationship was made known. In the meantime, he hoped they could carry on until the oil deal was signed.

"I hope you know what you're doing," Khalid said. "I'm off to the south for a few days. I want to check out the pipeline from the number four oil rig. There's a leak somewhere and so far no one's found it. If it catches fire, there'll be hell to pay." Khalid rose. "Maybe I should take the new jet and vet it for you."

"It's my new toy. Get one of your own."

Khalid's sarcastic snort of laughter conveyed his amusement. "Don't need one. I use the company's," he said, referring to the fleet of small aircraft the oil company owned.

"You don't have to have hands-on surveillance of the rigs," Rashid said. "And if there is a fire, let someone else deal with it."

"Hey, that's my job."

He and Khalid had this conversation a dozen times a month. He glanced at his brother, his gaze focused briefly on the disfiguring swath of scar tissue running from his right cheek down his neck to disappear beneath his shirt collar. The oil fire that had caused the damage had eventually been extinguished—by Khalid himself. The devastation hadn't stopped him from turning his back on office work and continuing in the oil fields. His elite company of oil firefighters was in high demand whenever an oil fire broke out.

Both of them had inherited wealth when their father had died. Both had a strong sense of obligation to the family oil business. Rashid preferred to hire competent help for routine tasks. He loved dealing in the world markets. But his twin had always found the drilling sites fascinating. Not to mention finding the conflagrations that could ruin a site a challenge to extinguish. Khalid drove their mother crazy with concern.

The phone rang.

"Did she arrive?" His mother's voice sounded in his ear.

Khalid gave a mock bow and left his brother to the phone call.

"My guest arrived and is staying at Grandmother's villa," Rashid said. Another front to deal with. His mother had been instrumental in the arrangement of the alliance with Haile. She herself had had an arranged marriage and she wanted her sons to follow the old ways.

"I can't wait to meet her. I know you were hesitant about this arrangement, but it'll work out for the best for all. Plan to bring her to dinner tonight."

"Ah, I believe you misunderstood me, Mother," he said. The charade started now. "Haile had other plans. My guest is Bethanne Sanders. Someone I know from Starcraft." When concocting a magnificent lie, it was best to stick as close to the truth as possible.

"What do you mean?" He heard the bewilderment in her tone.

"I will be happy to bring Bethanne to meet you tomorrow. For tonight, we wish to be together. She's had a long flight and is tired."

"But Haile? What of her?"

"I'll explain when we meet," he said.

"Rashid, don't be impetuous."

He almost laughed. It had been years since he'd been impetuous. His brief aborted love for Marguerite when he'd been younger had ended that streak. Now he kept careful control of his emotions and actions. "Rest assured, Mother, I do not plan to repeat the past."

When the call ended, he reached for the folder on the new jet. He needed to know more about the woman he had ensconced at the villa and quickly. His assistant had approved the requests for visas for both pilots. He took the photograph of Bethanne and stepped closer to the window, his curiosity raised. Blond hair, blue eyes, tall for a woman. A standard passport photo, yet the playfulness lurking in the depths of her blue eyes contrasted with the severe hairstyle, pulled back probably into a ponytail. He'd seen the anger flash in her eyes on the plane. And the shrewd bargaining to help find her father. Was Khalid right, she would be looking for some way to gain money or prestige from the charade?

She didn't look very old. Yet he knew she had to be experienced. Starcraft was an established firm that didn't take chances with the multimillion-dollar aircrafts it built.

How novel to have a woman pilot. Had that fact made the rumor mill yet? He put the photo back, wondering what the financial minister was making of the situation. Rashid had to make sure he did not learn the true circumstances until the deal was consummated. Or even then, if he could help it.

For a moment he remembered their meeting on the plane. She had caught his attention instantly. She was far different from anyone he knew. Wasn't it his luck she was off-limits because of her father. He would love to explore the attraction he felt when he first saw her standing proudly at the top of the stairs. But as the daughter of a thief, he could not let himself enjoy their relationship. He needed to be on guard for any nefarious activity on her part. The apple never fell far from the tree. Was she also not to be trusted?

Hank had worked for his father for many years when he stole the latest jet in their fleet. What had caused his actions? They'd probably never know unless they found him. But he'd watch his daughter. Their family would not be caught unawares a second time.

He was in a tight spot—balancing the minister on one hand, his mother's interest on another, and needing to keep his guest visible enough to satisfy curiosity, and secluded enough to insure she could not threaten the situation.

In addition, he was now committed to delving into the old business of the theft of their plane. Three years ago, when his father died, Rashid had stepped into his place at the oil company. Khalid had worked on locating Hank and the plane—with no tangible results. They'd accepted the loss and moved on. Would they have any more success now?

CHAPTER TWO

BETHANNE wondered how much of the beach she was walking on belonged to the sheikh. She had not seen any sign of other people as she walked, and she estimated she'd gone almost a mile. The water was warm on her feet. The sand swished around her toes as the spent waves swirled around them. She wished she'd worn a hat or something; the sun was burning hot on her head. She was reluctant to return, however. The walk was soothing and just touching the ground where her father might have once stood gave her a connected feeling that had been missing a long time. She could imagine she'd run into him and they'd both express surprise and immediately begin talking and catching up. Then she'd realize he'd been extremely busy and had not died alone and unlamented somewhere unknown, but had simply let time slip by. He had never done so before, but Bethanne clung to hope.

Finally she turned to retrace her steps. Glad she'd left her shoes above the tide line as an indicator of where to return, she studied the lush vegetation that bordered the beach. The villa was almost invisible from the shore. When she caught a glimpse of it, she also saw someone sitting in one of the chairs near the path.

Her heart rate increased as she walked closer. Even before she could recognize him, she knew it was Sheikh Rashid al Harum. Rashid. She said the name softly. He rose as she approached, watching her. Conscious of her windblown hair, sandy feet, khaki pants rolled up to her knees, she knew she must appear a sight. Why couldn't she have brought a dress that would look feminine and sexy? No, she had to be practical. What would he think?

"Did you enjoy your walk?" he asked.

She nodded, leaning over to roll down her pants and dust the sand off first one foot and then the other. Slipping on her shoes, she wished she had worn sandals. Glancing at her watch, she saw she'd been gone longer than she realized. It was approaching the dinner hour.

"It's quite lovely," she said, standing again. "I'd like to go swimming while I'm here."

"My brother and I enjoyed the beach when we were children. The villa used to belong to my grandmother. It's been a long time since I've gone swimming here."

End of conversation. She cast around for something else to say. But the topic she wanted to discuss was, of course, the charade he'd insisted upon. So—

"I don't think this is going to work," she said.

"Because?"

"I've had time to think about it. No one's going to believe you have fallen for some jet jockey from America. First of all, where would we have met? Then, let's face it, I'm no femme fatale."

His gaze skimmed over her. Bethanne felt her blood heat. She wished she could read minds. What did he think when he looked at her? When he again met her eyes, he smiled.

Bethanne's heart flipped over. The way his eyes crinkled with that smile had her fascinated. It changed his entire demeanor. He was the best-looking man she'd ever met. He had to know the effect he had on women. On her.

Flustered, she tried to appear unaffected, but suspected the color rising in her cheeks gave her away.

"You look like you could be most intriguing, with the right clothing."

"And that's another thing. I would not have come to visit bringing only uniforms and casual clothes! I expected to be searching for my father, not going anywhere where I needed to look like I could attract a sheikh."

He laughed. "Even in your casual clothes, people would know why you would attract a sheikh. But clothing is easily remedied. In fact, I took the liberty of having some dresses sent to your room. Please accept as a token of my appreciation for your help."

"Help? You practically kidnapped me." What had he meant by *people would know why you would attract a sheikh?* Did he like the way she looked?

"Hardly that. You agreed to help in exchange for my resuming the search for your father. I don't think we'll turn up anything at this late date, but I will make some inquiries."

Bethanne considered the terms. She was not going to stop believing in her father just on the sheikh's say-so. She knew her father would never betray anyone. Still, any help would be appreciated. "Okay, it's your party. If you think we can fool people, good luck."

"You underestimate yourself. No one will ever doubt that I could be interested."

"Nicely said. Maybe there is a ghost of a chance," she said. Her heart rate increased with his compliment. And the look in his eyes. Definite interest.

"Dinner will be served at seven. Perhaps you would join me on the veranda then?" he asked.

"Thank you, I should be delighted." She nodded regally and swept by, wishing she wore a lovely dress and didn't have sand chafing her feet.

Bethanne gazed at the closet full of clothes five minutes later. Rashid's last words echoed in her mind. No one could doubt he could be interested if she wore some of these dresses. How had he arranged to have so many different ones delivered in the few hours since he deposited her at the villa?

Duh, money can accomplish anything, she thought as she fingered the light silks and linens. She pulled out a blue dress that matched her eyes.

Pampering herself with a luxurious bath and then paying careful attention to her hair and makeup, Bethanne felt a bit like she'd imagine Cinderella felt dressing for the ball.

Fatima had knocked on the door as she was slipping on the dress. She smiled and nodded, saying something in Arabic that Bethanne didn't understand. But the universal signs of approval were obvious. What had the sheikh told this woman about their charade?

The blue of the dress did indeed enhance the color of her eyes. During her walk the sun had tinted her skin with a light tan and the constant hint of excitement at the thought of dining with a sheikh had her on tenterhooks and brought additional color to her cheeks.

Descending the stairs shortly before seven, she wished Rashid were at the bottom to see her descend. The designer dress hugged her figure and made her feel as sexy as a French movie star. She hoped it would replace the image he had of her windblown and disheveled from her walk.

Reaching the ground floor, she headed toward the sound of male voices. She entered a formal sitting room a moment later, just as the butler left. She took a deep breath, dismayed to find her stomach full of butterflies and her palms growing damp. Why this sudden attack of nerves? He was the same. Nothing had changed. But she felt as if the stakes had been rachetted up a notch. She had to find her father to prove his innocence. It became important that the sheikh not think she came from a dishonored family.

As if sensing her arrival, the sheikh turned.

"Thank you for the dress. It's more than expected and quite lovely," Bethanne said quickly, her words almost too fast to understand. Her heart rate tripled and she gripped her poise and tried to act as if she were comfortable greeting Arabian sheikhs every day.

"It is of no consequence. I hope your stay in Quishari will be enjoyable. If you need anything while here at the villa, do ask."

"I look forward to seeing Quishari while I'm here. Since I assume I'll have some free time while you're at work, perhaps you could recommend a guide who speaks English? If I can hire a car, I can explore on my own. I've heard so much about the country for years. I can't believe I'm here." Or at least under these circumstances. Her father had loved Quishari. She knew she would as well.

"I shall put one of my drivers and cars at your disposal. Do allow me to show you the major sights of my country. I am anxious to try out the plane. If you would fly it for me, we can put it through its paces tomorrow."

"I'd love to. I am at your service," she said, feeling almost giddy with the thought she might actually fly where her father had flown. And find time to talk to maintenance men who might know what happened to him. She was a bit surprised the al Harum family had not done more to pursue the issue. Had they merely dismissed it as casual theft and written off a plane? she wondered.

Perhaps in the greater scheme of things, it didn't cost much from their perspective. But she would have thought Rashid the type to go after someone who had done him wrong and make sure justice triumphed.

"Then I will see that you have every opportunity to explore. I'm quite proud of our heritage and history. Some of the architecture in the old section of town is renowned."

"I look forward to seeing it all." In truth, she never expected Rashid to spend a moment with her if not in a public forum in an attempt to discourage gossip.

"Did the dresses fit?"

She loved hearing that deep, melodious voice with its trace of British accent. Why were Americans such suckers for accents? Her Southern drawl sounded out of place in the posh cosmopolitan sitting room with elaborate brocade sofas and antiques dating back centuries.

"The ones I tried on fit perfectly. I loved this one the best."

"It was the color of your eyes," he said.

She caught her breath. Had he noticed enough to request this special color? She searched his eyes for a hint of the truth, but though he looked at her for a long moment, his expression gave nothing away. He'd be terrific at high-stakes poker.

"I thought from your visa photo that you seemed young to be an experienced pilot. Now it appears you're far too feminine to fly planes."

"I've had plenty of training." She didn't know whether to be flattered at the subtle compliment or defensive for her abilities. Did he think women weren't as capable as men to pilot aircrafts?

"You graduated from the U.S. Air Force Academy, took flight training and flew a number of fixed wing crafts and helicopters while serving," Rashid said. "I read your background sent from Starcraft."

"You needn't worry I can't handle your new jet."

He laughed, amusement dancing in his eyes. "I never

doubted it. You brought it safely from the United States. Come, dinner will be ready by now." He offered his arm to Bethanne. She took it, feeling awkward. She was more at ease in the casual restaurants she normally patronized than dining with an Arabian sheikh. But her experiences taught her how to meet every challenge—even this one.

Dinner proved to be less disconcerting than she'd expected. Once seated, the conversation centered around the new jet, its performance and the enhancements Rashid had ordered. After they ate, Rashid insisted they share hot tea on the veranda overlooking the garden. By the time it grew dark, Bethanne was glad to retreat to her bedroom. It had been a long day. One that had not ended as expected.

He bid her good-night at the foot of the stairs and even as she climbed them, he left the villa. The sound of his car faded as she shut her bedroom door.

Bethanne twirled around the large room in sheer joy. She felt as if she were a part of a fairy tale. Handsome sheikh, beautiful setting, lovely clothes and nothing to do but fly a plane at his whim. Could life be any better?

Falling asleep to the soft soughing of the sea relaxed Bethanne like nothing else. Before dropping off, she vowed she'd begin her search for her father tomorrow. But for tonight, she wanted to think about the dashing sheikh who chose her for his special guest—if only temporarily.

Minnah awakened Bethanne the next morning when she entered the bedroom carrying a tray of fragrant hot choco-late and a basket of fresh pastries and croissants. Breakfast in bed was not a luxury Bethanne enjoyed often and she plumped up her pillows and took the heavy silver tray on her lap with delight. There was an English newspaper folded neatly on one side.

"Thank you," she said as the woman went to the French doors to open them wide to the fresh morning breeze.

"I will bring you bathing suits after your breakfast. His Excellency suggested you'd like a swim before starting your day." The maid's English was practically flawless. "Later a driver will pick you up to take you to the airport. His Excellency is anxious to fly in the new plane."

"Sounds like a plan," Bethanne said, already savoring the rich dark chocolate taste of the hot beverage. The feeling of being a princess living in the height of luxury continued. But she dare not waste a moment.

"Before you leave," she said to Minnah, "did you know Hank Pendarvis? He was also a pilot for the sheikh. Or at least the oil company."

The maid tilted her head slightly as she tried to remember. Finally she shook her head slightly. "I do not know him."

That would have been too easy, Bethanne thought. She thanked her and resumed eating breakfast.

Selecting a one-piece blue swimsuit from her new wardrobe a short time later, she donned the accompanying cover-up and headed for the beach. A short swim would be perfect. It was warm enough to enjoy the water without the blazing heat that would rise later in the day. Fatima accompanied her. She had been informed of Bethanne's plans by the maid. For the time being, Minnah would act as the go-between. Bethanne wondered how she'd learned English. When they reached the beach, Fatima sat on one of the chairs near the edge, apparently content to watch from a distance.

Feeling pampered and spoiled, Bethanne relished each sensation as her day started so differently from normal. Shedding the cover-up near the chairs, she ran to the water, plunging in. It was warm and buoyant. Giving in to the pleasure the sea brought, she swam and floated and thoroughly enjoyed herself. She had a goal to reach and a job to do. But for a few moments, she felt carefree and happy.

At the airport an hour later, Bethanne's attitude changed from bemused delight to efficient commander. She talked to the ground crew through a translator the sheikh had provided, reviewing items on the checklist. She listened to how they had refueled the aircraft. She did a visual inspection of the jet. She wasn't sure when the sheikh would want to take the maiden flight, but she was ready when he was. Now she had nothing to do but await his arrival.

She beckoned the translator over. "Can you ask among the crew if any of them knew Hank Pendarvis? He was a pilot and probably flew from this airport," she said.

He nodded and walked back to the group of men.

Two spoke to his question and both looked over at Bethanne. Breaking away from the rest, the two men and the translator walked to her.

"These men knew him. He was a pilot for His Excellency's father, Sheikh Rabid al Harum."

"Is he dead?" she asked bluntly, studying the two men who had known her father.

One man looked away when the question was posed in Arabic. The other looked sad and shook his head at Bethanne, speaking rapidly.

"It is unfortunate, but it appears he has vanished. Was he a friend of yours?"

Bethanne didn't want to reveal her connection to all and sundry. "An acquaintance. I heard he had a job in Quishari and hoped to look him up while I am here."

There was lengthy conversation between the three men, with a couple of glances thrown her way as the one man grew quite passionate.

Finally the translator turned to her. "The man was a pilot. One day he took a plane without permission. He never returned. It is surmised he either flew to another country or the plane crashed. No one has heard from him in almost three years. And the plane has not flown over Quishari skies since then."

She wanted to protest that her father was not a thief, but these men confirmed what Rashid had said. But it couldn't be. Her father was nothing like that. He was loyal to the al Harum family. Loved his job. He would not risk it to steal a plane, no matter what the provocation.

"Did they search for a crashed plane?" she asked, holding on to her composure with effort. Had no one been concerned when he disappeared? Had they so quickly condemned him as a thief that no one searched in case there had been an accident? Her heart ached. Her father had to be dead. He would have contacted her long before now if he could have. She refused to believe he stole the plane.

Another bout of conversation and then one of the men shrugged and turned to walk back to the group. The other continued talking and then watched Bethanne when the translator told her a search was impossible when no one knew where he'd gone. The desert was vast, uninhabited for the most part. Without knowing the direction he'd taken, it was fruitless to search.

"And no one knew why he took the flight?" she asked. How far could she push without giving away her avid interest?

"He was pilot to the old sheikh who died shortly after the man disappeared. His son had no knowledge of the reason he took the plane. There is no more," he ended sadly.

"Thank you." She forced a smile at the man who had conveyed the information. Refusing to let her dismay show, she walked back to the plane.

She wished she had some time alone to assimilate the cold facts. What would have compelled her father to take a plane if not authorized? He hadn't owned a plane, just flew for whoever hired him. Where could he have been going? Why was there no debris if he'd crashed? Someone flying over an accident site must have seen it. Maybe he'd flown off the normal route. Maybe he had not filed a flight plan and no one knew where to look. Yet, how could he have flown without filing a plan? She'd had to fill out enough paper to fill a box when requesting routes into Quishari. Even this morning when saying she wanted to take the jet up, she'd had to fill out a half-dozen forms.

She entered the plane and wandered through the sumptuous cabin. The interior had been designed to the specifications requested by Rashid al Harum. She sat on the sofa, encased in comfort. The microsuede fabric was sensuous to the touch, feeling like velvet. The thick Persian rug on the floor felt sumptuous beneath her feet. She'd like to take off her shoes and scrunch her toes in the luxury. It was like a fine drawing room. The only time she flew, when not piloting an aircraft, she was crammed into the cheapest seats possible returning to base. What would it be like to fly high above the earth in such elegant furnishings? Nothing like the flights she knew.

For a moment she imagined herself sitting next to the sheikh as they cruised high above the Arabian desert. He'd offer her a beverage. They'd sit close together, heads bent toward each other, enjoying each other's company.

Rashid Al Harum entered, ducking his head slightly to clear the lintel. He looked surprised to see her.

Bethanne jumped to her feet instantly, her face growing warm with embarrassment. Bad enough to be daydreaming, but to be caught sitting as if she had nothing to do was problematic.

"I'm sorry. I just took a moment to test the sofa," she said in a rush. She had no business imagining herself as a guest aboard this lovely plane. She was here to work!

"And is it as comfortable as it looks?" he asked, taking her presence in the cabin of the plane instead of the cockpit with equanimity.

"Fabulous. The seat belts are discreet. I feel like I'm in a small living room somewhere. I hope it meets your expectations." She stepped toward the front of the plane, hoping to squeeze by, but his presence filled the narrow space.

"If you're ready to depart, I'll begin the preflight checklist," she said, overwhelmed a bit by his proximity. It wasn't only his sheer masculinity, which made her feel quite feminine, it was the way he carried himself—with all the confidence in the world. And his good looks would give anyone a run for his money. Tall, dark and handsome was such a cliché—and now Bethanne knew exactly why. He looked like the dream of every young woman anywhere with his fabulous features, dark hair and chiseled lips that she'd like to touch hers just once.

Get a grip, girl, she admonished herself. They would never have met in other circumstances. And the only thing he wanted to touch was the fancy furnishing of his new jet. Or the signed copy of the contract for the deal he was working on.

To further her efforts to return to reality instead of indulging in fantasy, she reminded herself the man thought her father a thief. But instead of putting a damper on things, it strengthened her resolve to find her father to clear his name. For his sake, and for hers. She wanted Rashid to think well of her no matter what.

He stepped aside and Bethanne squeezed by, careful to make sure she didn't touch however much tempted. Breathless with the encounter, she hurried to the pilot's seat and sank down, grateful for the few moments' solitude. She ran through the preflight checklist in the cockpit, hoping she could concentrate on flying and not have her mind winging its way back to the cabin and the sexiest man she'd ever encountered.

"Ready when you are," Rashid said, slipping into the second seat a few minutes later.

"You want to fly up here?" she squeaked.

"Why wouldn't I? Wouldn't a man want to spend time with his special friend?"

She glanced out the window at the scurry of activity in preparation for departure. The ground crew could easily see into the cockpit. Of course he wanted to bolster the conception they were involved.

"Okay. Ever flown up front before?"

"From time to time."

In only minutes they were shooting into the sky, the power of the rear engines thrusting them effortlessly into the air. Bethanne had no trouble focusing on the controls. The best part of everything was soaring above the earth. She had calculated the route south along the coast and had it approved by ground control. Flying for one of the top businessmen in the country gave her special privileges not normally afforded.

Slowly Bethanne leveled out and then gradually climbed to their cruising altitude. She prided herself on her smooth flights. The smaller planes were more susceptible to variations in air currents. Today was all about showing off how smoothly the jet rode.

Once they reached cruising level, Rashid nodded. "Good ride."

For a few moments, she'd forgotten he was there. Now, suddenly the space seemed to shrink. The scent of aftershave lotion the sheikh used tickled her nose and made her heart beat faster. She kept her eyes ahead, but could still envision every inch of his face as if he had put a photograph in front of her.

"Do you fly?" she asked.

"No. I leave that to the experts. But I sit up here with my pilot sometimes. I like the panoramic views which I don't get from only one side of the airplane. And I like the feeling of freedom. Must be one reason you enjoy it."

"The primary reason, I guess. It's fabulous." She wished her pulse would slow.

"Unusual profession for a woman, at least in Quishari."

"Not that many women pilots in the U.S., but we're growing in numbers."

"Did you always want to fly?"

She nodded. "From when I was a little girl. It was always magical to me. Soaring high above the earth. My dad—" She stopped abruptly. "Sorry, I'm rambling on."

"If I didn't want to learn more, I wouldn't have asked the question. Your father got you interested?"

She nodded stiffly, still feeling raw with what she'd learned this morning. She wanted to defend him to the sheikh. But she had only a daughter's loyalty to offer. She needed more facts.

"I, too, am following in my father's footsteps. He and my uncles built the oil company to the stature it is today before they died. The loss of them has been a tragedy for my family. My father built an empire through hard work and integrity. My brother and I and one remaining uncle are hoping to build it to even new levels."

"Lofty plans. From what I know, Bashiri Oil is already a leader."

"I hope to be remembered as my father is—someone with vision and the ability to achieve results."

Rashid was charming, Bethanne thought to herself. It was probably second nature to him, which would go a long way in achieving his ends.

"So how is our charade going? No accusations of impossibility?" she asked.

"No one would dare question my word," he said.

"Good."

"My mother expects us for dinner tonight. I accepted on behalf of both of us."

"She'll spot the incongruity."

"I fully expect her to question you about everything. It's up to you to make sure you allay any suspicions. One thing to keep in mind, if she discovers who your father was, she will never believe the relationship."

She resented his suggesting she would be less than worthy of being considered as a wife for the sheikh because of her father.

"I have done nothing wrong. And I don't believe my father has, either."

"Nevertheless, don't volunteer that information."

The sooner she found out the truth, the better, Bethanne fumed.

"Down there, circle around," he said.

Spotting a chain of oil rigs off the shore, she angled down slightly. "Are those the rigs you wanted to see?" One in the distance seemed to shimmer in the heat, gold flames reaching high. "Is that one on fire?" she asked in disbelief as they flew closer.

"Damn. I was hoping it wasn't. If Khalid is in the midst of it, I'll skin him alive."

She blinked at the vehemence of his tone. Who was Khalid? Did Rashid suspect the man had started the fire?

She contacted air traffic control to alert them to her altered plan, then began a wide sweep to the right around the chain of derricks. The last one in the line billowed flames, easily seen from their height. How frightening it would be if they were closer.

"How do you put out oil fires?" she asked, keeping a distance from where the heated air would be rising. Even at this distance they rocked slightly from the thermals.

"Best left to the experts. Which Khalid is. Not that it's any guarantee of his safety."

"And Khalid is?" she asked quietly, taking in his tenseness as he stared at the scene below.

"My brother."

"Oh."

Bethanne made the wide circle twice, then Rashid told her to return to the airport. "I need a phone."

"Don't forget this aircraft is equipped with the latest in satellite technology," she said, feeling a bit like an ad on television.

"I had, thank you." He rose and headed for the back of the plane.

"Whoosh," Bethanne said, feeling the atmosphere around her grow lighter with him gone. She hoped Khalid wasn't in the thick of things or he was sure to get the full brunt of his brother's anger.

How odd that his brother fought fires. They had more than enough money to hire the best. Why put his life on the line?

She wished she knew more about Rashid and his family. Her father had held the family in high esteem. He had enjoyed working for them, although he hadn't told her much about them. She couldn't deny she was attracted to the man, but it would be wiser to ignore that attraction. Where did she think it could lead? The pretense would end once Rashid finalized his important deal.

A short while later, she lined up the jet on the glide path the tower indicated. The landing was as smooth as silk. She taxied to the hangar and cut the engines.

"Now what?" she wondered aloud as she began the end of her light checklist.

"You return to the villa, I to work," Rashid said from the door. "Nice flight, thank you."

Bethanne felt a rush of pleasure at his words. Not every

multigazillionaire even noticed the people who worked for him, much less offered any praise for a job well done.

"Nice aircraft," she responded. "Were you able to use the phone feature?"

"It worked perfectly. The ride was comfortable. The appointments are just as I wanted. I'm sure I'll have years of use from it."

Bethanne pictured him lounging in the cabin for flights around the Middle East or as far as Europe. This model was the best plane Starcraft produced and she was pleased the buyer seemed satisfied.

"Was your brother at the fire?"

"Yes, and says he has it under control."

"Scary job."

"Dangerous, too. I have instructed one of my drivers, Teaz Suloti, to drive you wherever you wish while visiting. Teaz speaks English. Of course, you have complete use of the villa. The library has a number of books in English."

"Thank you."

"I'll pick you up at six-thirty tonight. We'll dine with my mother at her place at seven."

"Right. Shouldn't I know more about you if we're pretending to be involved?"

"Like?"

"Oh, come on. People who know each other and are attracted to each other want to know more about the other person. The early stages are questions and reminiscences and all. Did I misunderstand or do you want people to think we are on the brink of an engagement?"

"You are correct. I had forgotten."

"Forgotten what?"

"How people who are involved act."

She frowned. "I'm not sure I follow."

"Nothing you need be concerned with. I'll come earlier than planned and brief you on important parts."

"So I should have a dossier on myself prepared as well?" she asked.

"Not necessary. We have information on your visa request. I can wing the rest."

Bethanne settled back into the luxury seats of the limousine a few moments later, wishing she could have continued to spend time with the sheikh—if only to listen to his deep voice with its pleasing accent. She also had a bunch of questions. She knew so little about the man. She couldn't face his mother and not give away the show. She hoped he knew what he was doing.

When they reached the villa, she'd ask about her father to everyone she came into contact with on the sheikh's staff. Someone must have befriended him. He had a sparkling wit and genuine interest in people and places. Had they all condemned him without a fair hearing?

When they reached the villa, the driver opened the door and stood by, waiting for her to get out.

Once on the pavement, Bethanne stopped and looked at Teaz. "Did you know Hank Pendarvis?" she asked.

For a few seconds he made no move or response. Then he nodded abruptly—once.

"Do you know what happened to him?"

"He was the pilot for the old sheikh. He flew away one day and never returned." His English was heavy with Arabic accent, but Bethanne had no trouble understanding him.

"Do you know where he was going?"

The same stare, then a quick shake of his head.

"Thank you," she said. She started for the front door when a thought occurred. Turning, she saw Teaz still staring at her. "Do you know where he lived?"

"In the Romula section of old town."

She waited, hoping for more, but he said nothing. She had the address. Might as well go and see if she could find someone there who knew him.

"Maybe you could drive me there tomorrow if the sheikh doesn't need me." She'd love to see the old city. Match photos with the historic buildings. See a square with coffee cafés and stalls of goods for sale. Skirting Alkaahdar from the airport to the villa showed only the modern high-rises of shining steel and glass. She knew the older section would have been built in the more traditional Moorish architecture that she'd so loved in southern Spain.

"I am at your service," he said with a slight bow.

Entering the quiet villa, Bethanne paused at the bottom of the steps, then on a sudden whim turned and headed toward the sitting room she'd been in last night. A quick glance showed it empty. Moving down the wide hall, she peered into the dining room they'd used. The last room in the hall was the library the sheikh had mentioned. Books lined three walls. The French doors stood open, keeping the room fresh and cool. Stepping inside, she saw a large desk to one side. From the computer on top and the scattered papers, she knew it had been recently used. Who by? From their conversation, she'd surmised Rashid lived elsewhere. This was a second home.

She stepped in and crossed to the desk. She wouldn't open drawers and nothing was visible that would tell her anything about her father. It had been three years. Time enough to put away anything of interest.

"Where did you go, Dad? And why?" she muttered softly.

She sat in the desk chair, picturing Rashid sitting behind the desk, working on major deals for oil exports. What did he do for leisure? How come he was not married at his age? Most men she knew had married in their twenties. Rashid had to be close to mid-thirties.

Though she herself was still unwed.

She swiveled back and forth in the chair. Spotting the computer, she sat up and turned it on. Maybe she could search out what she could find about Rashid al Harum. She would not go to dinner unprepared.

Rashid leaned back as the car pulled away from the office. He was on his way to pick Bethanne up for the command dinner. He had thought about her questions, wondering what she felt important to know if preparing for a confrontation with a future mother-in-law.

He thought about Marguerite for the first time in years. How foolish he'd been not to recognize her type when they'd met. He'd fallen for her in a big way. Marguerite had been beautiful and sophisticated and very good at having fun. She'd often spoken about how much fun they'd have together.

Spending his money.

How gullible he'd been. No longer. He had agreed to the possibility of marriage to Haile as a way to connect the two families who had a strong mutual interest in oil. Now that was off the table, he could resume his solitary way of life. It would take another monumental deal to have him consider the institution again soon.

Lucky break, Haile's running away.

He wondered if his mother would ever see it that way. He'd have to be careful in what he conveyed to her this evening. She could accept things or constantly stir things up in her desire for answers.

How good an actress was Bethanne Sanders? Could he depend upon her? How ironic the woman he was looking to for help was the daughter of a man his family despised.

If she was anything like her father, he was playing a dangerous game.

He entered the villa a short time later and paused in the large foyer. The stairs leading up were to his left. The space to the right led to various rooms and eventually back to the kitchen. The evening breeze circulated, keeping the house cool and inviting. Why didn't he stay here more often? he wondered. His grandmother had left it to him when she died last summer. She'd bequeathed another dwelling and surrounding land on the other side of the city to his twin. Khalid had yet to take up residence. Both too busy.

Fatima started down the stairs, surprised to see him. "I didn't know you were here, Excellency," she said. She clung to the railing and looked back up. "I can tell her you have arrived."

"Please ask her to join me in the salon."

Rashid waited by one of the French doors. The entire estate was cooler than his flat in the city. He liked living closer to the action, but he had forgotten how much he'd enjoyed visiting when his grandmother was alive. Only a few minutes' drive from the heart of the capital, yet the estate was serene and lovely, and quite different from the glass and steel of the high-rise where he had his flat.

When he heard the rustle of silk, he turned and watched as Bethanne entered the room. She looked lovely in a rose-colored dress that was most demure. Her hair was done in a neat style, up and off her neck. She wore no jewelry, but her modest attire would please his mother.

"Good evening," she said with a bright smile. For a moment Rashid wished she meant the smile, that she was actually happy to see him. It was a foolish, fleeting thought.

"You look lovely," he said.

"Thank you—it's the dress." She turned slowly and

grinned. "I could get used to dresses like this. Most of the time I wear my uniform or shorts when hanging around at home."

He'd like to see her in shorts or a bathing suit. Or nothing at all.

Looking away quickly lest he give a hint of his errant thoughts, he walked to one of the chairs and gestured for her to sit in another.

She did so elegantly. What were the odds of having a suitable woman arrive just when Haile disappeared? One who seemed as at home here in his villa as she did behind the controls of the jet?

"So let the inquisition begin," he said whimsically.

She shrugged. "I looked you up on the Internet. There's quite a lot written about you and your brother. You have a lot of good press. Is that designed? Or are you genuine?"

"I'd like to say genuine. We are not given to excesses. We enjoy our work and do our best for it."

"Your brother is harder to find out about, but you are often in the press. But no special woman—hence the arrangement with Miss Haile, I suppose."

He kept his face without expression. At least the old press about his and Marguerite's disastrous breakup was old news, probably not in the top articles brought up when his name was entered in a search engine. He had his father to thank for that.

"So I know more about you than this morning. Enough to fool your mother? That I'm not sure. There's not much personal, like what your favorite food is or if you had a dog when you were a child."

He relaxed. She was not probing for intimate details, just basic facts.

"My favorite food is candied dates. My brother and I had a wonderful dog when we were children. I miss him to this day. But my life is too busy and hectic to have a pet."

She settled and began a litany of questions, firing them off as if on an invisible checklist—favorite book, movie, activity, color. Did he consider himself close to his family? Did he have special friends she should know about? A hobby that consumed him? How had he done in school? What did he like about his job and what did he wish to change? Who did he admire most in the world?

It was a novel experience to be so questioned. Not once did she ask about material things.

Finally she stopped. "Ready as I'll ever be," she said, looking as if she were about to jump to her feet.

Rashid looked at her. "My turn."

"I thought you had all you needed from the report Starcraft sent," she said, looking amused.

"Ah, but I didn't realize all the nuances of information necessary for an almost-engaged couple's knowledge bank. I do not know your favorites or your passions."

"Favorite color—blue. Food, anything with dark chocolate. Passions—flying. I have no boyfriend, which is lucky for you or we couldn't be doing this stupid charade. I am not close to my mother—nor the man she married after she divorced my father when I was little. I love traveling and seeing the world. I have experience shooting down other aircraft."

She looked adorable as she recited her list ending proudly with her startling fact. He was fascinated by the play of emotions across her face. Now sitting on the edge of her chair, her animation was a delight. Would his mother like her? What was not to like? As long as she didn't find out Bethanne's father's name.

"I hope there will be no need of the latter while you are in Quishari."

She laughed aloud. "I should hope never again, but it was training I received and just knowing I could do it improves my confidence. If I get into situations that make me uncomfortable, I remember I could shoot down a plane if needed and probably no one else in the room could."

"A strange way to improve confidence."

"It'll help when meeting your mother."

He laughed at that. This American woman was intriguing. He had even more reason to thank Haile for fleeing. If nothing else, Rashid planned to enjoy the next few days with Bethanne by his side. Without expectations on either part, they were free to enjoy the other's company without looking for hidden nuances or motives.

He rose. "Come, we'll be late if we don't leave soon. And tardiness is something my mother does not like."

"Tell me about her—I want her to be satisfied with the story we tell. Will she be hurt when the truth comes out?"

"Why should the truth ever come out?" he asked.

She looked at him in surprise. "Truth always comes out. You just make sure you put the right spin on it so she's not hurt by your deception."

"I would do nothing to hurt my mother."

"Good answer."

They were soon ensconced in the limo and on their way to the city.

"Where does your mother live?" Bethanne asked.

"In a penthouse apartment near the heart of the city, overlooking parts of the old section. She loves being in the center of things. It helps being close to friends since my father died."

"The soup is delicious," Bethanne said later, sipping the savory concoction. "So far I'm really enjoying the food here. I have a real sweet tooth and the candied walnuts really appeal. I shall have to buy a large package to take home when I leave."

Madame al Harum looked at her.

"And when do you leave?" she asked.

Bethanne smiled and glanced at Rashid. "Not for a long time, I hope."

She also hoped she was playing the role assigned her to his satisfaction. She'd been as gracious as she knew how when meeting his mother. She could tell at once that Madame al Harum did not like her. For one thing, she seemed to disapprove of tall, willowy blondes. She probably wanted a proper Arab woman for her son.

Then she expressed dismay that Bethanne was a pilot. It was too dangerous and too unseemly for a woman. Bethanne decided not to mention shooting down planes. She knew his mother would not appreciate that tidbit.

Dinner was easier. The food took some attention. She counted the minutes until they could finish and leave.

"And where is home for you?" the older woman asked.

"Galveston, Texas, right on the water. Galveston's an island that has been home all my life."

"What does your father do?"

"He's an antique dealer. But I have to say, history in Texas doesn't go back as far as here in Quishari. The old part of the capital city is thousands of years old. Texas has only been around for a few hundred years."

Rashid looked as if he were enjoying the meal. But Bethanne didn't think she was winning Brownie points with his mother.

"Tell me how you became interested in flying," Rashid said when the main course was served.

Grateful for the change of topic, Bethanne plunged right in.

"My father loved to fly and took me up in small planes almost as soon as I could sit up by myself." She smiled in memory. "It seemed logical when I got older that I, too, would love to fly. I actually learned when I was a teenager, to my mother's dismay. When I was accepted to the Academy, she really flipped. But I think Dad talked her in to letting me choose my own way. Anyway, I learned to fly a variety of air-crafts and here I am."

"So your father taught you to fly?" Rashid asked.

"No. That I had to do on my own. He was away more than home, actually. Probably why I'm following in his footsteps and seeing the world." She met his eye, holding it for a moment, silently refuting his ideas about her father.

"And that was your reason for choosing to attend a military academy?"

His mother's eyes grew large at that.

"Some of the recruitment material said join up and see the world. I knew I'd have the best education and pilot's training available. And I had a variety of aircraft to train on. I loved learning. And the service requirement enabled me to see Minot, North Dakota, in the dead of winter. Then a tour of Alaska. Can you imagine? I'm one who loves the sun and sea, and my two duty stations were the coldest in the U.S. I left the service when my commitment was up and landed a spot with Starcraft."

Rashid enjoyed watching Bethanne talk. He glanced at his mother. She had on that polite face she wore when tolerating others, but not connected to them. He felt a twinge of com-passion for her. She would have been so happy to have Haile sitting where Bethanne was sitting. She had met the woman on a trip to Morocco and had definitely approved of her.

He had seen pictures. She was a pretty woman. But not striking as Bethanne was. And he doubted she'd have shown much personality around his mother.

What would be his mother's reaction when he told her about Haile's fleeing? Nothing would bring her more happiness than to see one of her sons married—especially to a woman she liked. The fact he was the eldest—by seven minutes—made it seem as if the destiny of his family rested on his shoulders. One day he would have to marry—to father the next generation. He pushed aside the thought. As soon as the deal with al Benqura was finalized, he'd tell his mother Bethanne hadn't turned out to be the one for him after all. Maybe he'd even ask her help in finding him a suitable bride. Being a grandmother would delight her, he was sure.

"Tell me about North Dakota," he invited. "The only time I see snow is when we ski in Switzerland."

He was charmed by her storytelling skills. She made her experiences seem amusing while also revealing her reactions to different situations. She was skilled at entertaining and in giving him what he wanted—a devoted companion intent on meeting his needs. He hoped his mother saw her in that light. For a little while he could imagine what life would be like married to Bethanne. Never boring, of that he was sure.

She was having way too much fun, Bethanne thought at one point. This man was being polite in asking questions so she could talk, but she didn't need to give them her life's history—though Rashid did seem to be enjoying her rendition of her brief stint as an Air Force pilot. His mother looked rather horrified.

Glancing around, she could hardly believe she was sitting in an elegant penthouse overlooking the capital city. The furnishings were amazing. She wished her stepfather could see them. And surrounding the penthouse was a spacious terrace that had banks of pots with fragrant flowers. The doors were opened to allow the breeze to enter. It was delightful.

"You have a beautiful home," she said to her hostess. She had to find common ground or this dinner would end awkwardly.

Madame al Harum inclined her head regally. "I decorated

it for my husband. He loved to retreat from the world and find a place of beauty." She glanced at her son. "It's important that two people have much in common to make a happy marriage."

Bethanne also looked at Rashid. His mother wasn't buying their supposed commitment at all. Would he tell her now?

"Similar likes and dislikes, certainly," Rashid said. "But there is something to be said about learning about each other as the years go by, and have enough differences to be interesting."

His mother gave Bethanne a sour look and then nodded to her son. "That is important as well."

The rest of the meal processed without much comment. Bethanne was glad this was only a charade. She would not like being married into a family where the mother didn't like her. Or was it only because of her disappointment Haile hadn't come?

They did not stay long after dinner finished.

The ride back to the villa was completed in almost total silence. Bethanne knew Rashid had to be regretting his impetuous suggestion about their charade. Perhaps he'd end it tonight. The thought depressed her.

To her surprise, Rashid did not simply leave her at the door.

"It's early yet. If you are not tired, perhaps a few minutes on the veranda," he suggested.

"That would be nice. So do we change the charade now that we both know your mother doesn't like me?"

"My mother does not dictate my life. She is annoyed I didn't bring Haile tonight. She was instrumental in making that arrangement."

"It's more than that. She doesn't like me. Not just because I'm not Haile, but because of who I am," Bethanne said. She didn't need everyone in the world to like her, but she was a bit hurt Rashid's mother found her wanting.

"It's of no account," he said.

Of course not. This wasn't real. It was make-believe—

until he had his huge deal signed and sealed. Then she'd be on the next plane to Texas and his life would resume its normal course. Gossip would be quelled. He'd get his way and his mother would be very relieved.

"Her home was lovely," she said, looking for conversation. "Did you grow up there?"

"There and here and other places."

He looked out at the garden, visible now by the discreet lighting illuminating paths and special plants. He could hear the soft sound of the sea, noticeably different from faint traffic noise. "My flat today is not as pretty as this estate. It's downtown, not far from Mother's. I like living there yet I had almost forgotten how enjoyable this place is."

"Well, I appreciate being allowed to stay here. It's so much better than a hotel."

"I'm sure my grandmother would have been delighted to have visitors enjoy her home. She spent several months a year here. But had other property, as well."

Well, duh, Bethanne thought. His family probably had two dozen residences among them. She wondered idly if there were enough bedrooms among all the residences for him to sleep in a different one each night of the month. What must that feel like?

She had a sudden longing for her small apartment, with its familiar furnishings and photos. It might be fun to consider being Cinderella, but at the end of it all, wasn't she happier in her own home?

As Bethanne prepared for bed some time later, she thought about the evening. It would not have been better for Rashid's mother to welcome her into the family. She was not truly involved. And if the woman had liked her, she would have been disappointed when the charade was exposed.

Talking with Rashid on the veranda had given her a glimpse of what life married to him could be like. Only—there was no good-night kiss. She sighed softly. Was she going to be disappointed with no kiss before returning home? Yes. Yet she wasn't bold enough to kiss him.

Before turning off the lights, she opened the French doors to let the sea breeze sweep in. The light curtains billowed. The scents and fragrances from the garden were a delight. She slipped between cool sheets and lay down.

An hour later Bethanne was still wide awake. She'd tried lying on one side then the other, then flat on her back. Nothing worked. If she had a book or magazine to read, it might lead to sleep. She considered the situation, then sighed and got up. She had not brought a robe, thinking she'd be alone in a hotel room and not need one. Quietly she dressed in her slacks and shirt. Bare feet would be okay, she was sure. It was unlikely she'd run into anyone. It was after eleven. Surely all the staff had retired for the night.

She opened the door and stuck her head out, struck suddenly with the romantic-comedy picture that flashed into her mind. People sneaking from one room to another, peering into the hall to make sure the coast was clear. She planned nothing of the sort and stepped boldly out. She walked down the stairs, surprised when she reached the foyer to see a light coming from the library.

Silently she walked to the doorway. When she was within hearing distance she heard a phone. It was answered before the second ring.

The words were in Arabic, but she recognized Rashid's voice. She thought he had left long ago. When he'd bid her good-night, he said he had to pick up something from the library.

He was still here, and the phone call wasn't going well— not if the terse tone was anything to go by. She hesitated at the doorway, not wishing to interrupt, but still wanting something to read. She'd come this far; she'd wait for the conclusion of the call and then step in to find a book.

The conversation didn't take as long as she'd expected before a harsh word was sounded, then a string of them. She wondered what was going on. He sounded angry. Sudden silence ended the call.

When the silence had lasted several minutes, she took a breath and stepped closer, knocking slightly on the door frame. She saw him standing by open French doors. His back was ramrod straight. His body seemed to radiate strong emotion in contrast to the stillness with which he held himself.

He spun around, glaring at her for a second. Then he quickly adjusted his expression to reveal nothing.

"Something wrong?" he asked.

"I was going to ask you the same thing. I thought you left a while ago."

"I did. Then I remembered a file I had left and returned for it. I was about to leave when I got a phone call on my mobile phone." He still held it in his hand.

"I heard. Not that I understood a word, but it didn't sound like a very friendly call."

"It was from al Benqura. He found out about Haile. She contacted him. He was angry with me for not letting him know."

"How awkward that would have been."

Rashid sighed and walked back to the desk, leaning against it and nodding. "Awkward for him. He's threatening to end the deal. I told him in no uncertain terms that would not be acceptable unless he never wanted dealings with anyone in Quishari again."

Bethanne could empathize with the father whose daughter had run away and put him in a difficult situation. She watched as Rashid gradually relaxed. He was quick to anger, but also quick to regain his equilibrium. She saw when his curiosity was piqued by her arrival.

"What are you doing here?" His gaze dropped to her bare feet. His lips curved in a slight smile.

"I came for a book to read. I can't seem to sleep. You said you had some English books—I thought I'd get one of those."

He nodded and gestured to the shelving on the left. "English books on that wall. My grandmother used to entertain several friends from Great Britain. She has an assortment. The mysteries are on the lower shelves."

She crossed, conscious of his regard, and began to scan the titles. Finding a couple that sounded promising, she drew them from the shelf. Had Rashid read them? Could they discuss them after she finished?

Deciding to take both, she hugged them to her chest as she turned to face him.

"Now what?" she asked.

"You read them and fall asleep?" he asked.

"I mean with our charade. Did the phone call help or change things?"

"We continue. Whichever way the winds blow, we will adapt."

CHAPTER THREE

"I DON'T mean to intrude. But if you need someone to talk to, I could listen." She wished she'd had someone to listen to her when her father's disappearance became known. Her mother had long ago divorced herself from Hank Pendarvis—both legally and emotionally. She and Bethanne's stepfather had a loving and happy marriage from which Bethanne had often felt excluded. Plus, they never had a kind word to say about her father. Bethanne wished she could have him give her one of his bear hugs again. Did Haile's father feel that way?

"Did he hear from Haile?" she asked.

"He did. And is furious with her and with me."

"You're the injured party—why is he angry with you?"

"He believes I should have told him immediately. He could have taken steps. He overrates his power. By the time I found out, Haile had had hours to flee Morocco. She and her lover were married in Marseilles that very day. My telling him would not have prevented that."

"Will he tell others? Your minister?"

"Not if he wants this deal to go through."

He pushed away from the desk. "I have my folder. I won't keep you up any longer."

He looked at her slacks and T-shirt.

"Was sleeping attire not included in the clothes I ordered?"

"Yes, but no robe. I didn't know whom I might see if I came down for books."

"I shall remedy that in the morning."

"Please, I'm fine. Next time I'll take a book up with me. You've been more than generous. I don't need anything else."

"I thought all women loved beautiful things."

"I expect we do. But we don't have to own everything we see. Good night, Rashid."

Reaching her room a minute later, she softly closed the door and flung herself on the bed, the books falling on the mattress beside her. She had not expected to see him again tonight. He'd looked tired and somewhat discouraged. Not the best way to end a day. She hoped the deal would be signed soon. There was nothing else she could do but go along and hope in some small part she'd contribute to a satisfactory conclusion to their negotiations.

Trying to settle into a fictitious mystery when she had a real-life scenario in her own life was difficult. Murder was not involved in her case, but finding clues was. She tried to glean ideas from the book, but her mind turned time and time again to Rashid.

She knew he believed Hank to be a thief, but wouldn't he still want answers? Letting the book fall onto her chest, she gazed at the dark night beyond the billowing curtains. The man at the airport had said the son had no idea why her father took the plane. Didn't he want to know? She couldn't picture Rashid ignoring the situation. He'd push until he got answers.

Just before she fell asleep, she pictured herself with Rashid finding her father and finding the reason for the apparent theft. It could be explained away. Then Rashid would look at her with admiration and sweep her into his arms for a kiss….

She stopped herself—she had to stop fantasizing about his kisses!

Once again Minnah woke Bethanne the next morning, bringing a breakfast tray. The hot chocolate was as rich and satisfying as the previous day. The croissants were warm and buttery, melting in her mouth.

She debated going for a swim, but decided she had best set to searching for her father. She wanted to prove to Rashid his belief was misplaced.

"Pardon, I almost forgot," Minnah said after she opened the French doors and curtains to allow the sunshine to flood the room. "It is a letter from His Excellency. I will return for the tray in a while." She handed Bethanne an ivory-colored envelope with her name written in a bold script.

She opened it and read the brief note, her heart revving up. It had taken ages to fall asleep and then her dreams about Rashid had been exciting and most certainly not ones she wanted to share with anyone. The best favor she could do herself would be to remember always that this was merely make-believe.

A car will be at your disposal today. The driver will be waiting when you are ready to take you where you wish. He speaks English, and can translate if you wish to stop to shop or have coffee.

Disappointment warred with relief at the missive. What had she expected? A love note? An offer to spend the day with her?

The bold handwriting continued: *Saturday I have a polo match, I would like you to attend. Perhaps you'd care to see the horses before the game. If there is not a suitable dress for you to wear, let the maid know and she'll relay the information and something appropriate will be ordered.*

Bethanne was almost giddy with excitement. Trying not to act like a schoolgirl with a major crush, she took a deep breath. Of course someone being in a position of special guest would want to attend the polo match. Mentally she reviewed the new clothes. She wasn't entirely certain what was suitable for a polo match, but didn't think any of the lovely dresses were the right kind.

Still, the thought of his buying more clothes caused a pang. He didn't need to spend so much on this charade.

"Get real," she said aloud. "He can afford it and the clothes can go to some worthy cause when I leave."

Pushing the thought of leaving away, she quickly finished breakfast, showered and dressed in a light tan linen skirt and soft yellow cotton blouse. She planned to take advantage of the driver the sheikh offered to see some of the sights of old town this morning. She couldn't wait to see the ancient buildings, walk where generations past had walked. And maybe find out more about her father.

Then, if time permitted, she'd take advantage of the beauty of the Persian Gulf and laze on the beach until Rashid came after work.

Bethanne was pleased to see the driver at her disposal was the same one she'd asked about her father. She greeted him and told him of her desire to see the old city, and where Hank had lived.

When they arrived, he pulled into the curb and stopped.

"I cannot take the car any farther. The road becomes too narrow. Down there two blocks." He handed her a sheet of paper with Arabic writing. "I wrote his name and when he lived there and where. Show it to people for information about

Hank. Many speak some English. If not, come get me to translate. I will wait with the car."

"Thank you."

"You will not get a good reception," he warned.

"Why not?" That thought had never crossed her mind.

"The old sheikh was well liked. It was not a good thing to steal his plane. Some speculate the pilot's betrayal caused the heart attack that killed him. The man had flown the sheikh for years. His treachery cut deep."

Bethanne recognized she was fighting an uphill battle to clear her father's name. He would not have treated his employer that way—she knew it. His letters and phone calls had been full of admiration and respect for his employer. But how to prove that, and find out what really happened?

When she climbed out of the car, she was instantly in a foreign world. The tall sandstone walls were built closer to each other than most American buildings. Rising fifteen to twenty feet in height, they seemed to encase the street. Archways, windows and doors opened directly onto the narrow sidewalks, most already shuttered against the day's rising heat.

Bethanne was almost giddy with delight. She'd longed to visit Quishari ever since her father had first spoken about it. He had loved it and she knew she would as well. Savoring every moment, she slowly walked along, imagining she heard the echo of a thousand years. The heat shimmered against the terra cotta–colored walls. Here and there bright colors popped from curtains blowing from windows, or painted shutters closed against the heat.

She got her bearings and headed in the direction indicated in the drawing. Where the street intersected another, she peered down the cross streets, seeing more of the same. Archways had decorative Arabic writings. Recessed doorways intrigued, beckoned. For the most part, however, the reddish-brown of sandstone was the same. How did anyone find their own place when they all looked alike? she wondered.

Reaching a square, she was pleased with the wide-open area, filled with colorful awnings sheltering stalls with everything imaginable for sale. There were booths of brass, of glass, of luscious and colorful material and polished wood carvings. Some stalls sold vegetables, others fruit or flowers. Women and children filled the aisles. The sounds of excited chattering rose and fell as she looked around. On the far side, tables at two outside cafés crowded the sidewalk. Men in traditional Arab dishdashahs with white gitrahs covering their hair sat drinking the strong coffee. Others wore European attire. Several women dressed all in black stood near the corner talking, their string bags ladened with fresh produce from the stands in the square. The air was almost festive as shoppers haggled for the best bargain and children ran and played.

Bethanne watched in awe. She was actually here. Looking around, she noticed she was garnering quite a bit of attention. Obviously a curiosity to the daily routine. She approached one of the women and showed her the paper. The woman began talking in Arabic and pointing to a building only a few steps away. Bethanne thanked her, hoped she was pointing out the apartment where her father had lived. She quickly crossed there. No one responded to her knock.

Turning, she explored the square, stopping to ask in several of the stalls if anyone had known Hank Pendarvis, showing the paper the driver had prepared. No success until she came to one of the small sidewalk cafés on the far side of the square. A waiter spoke broken English and indicated Hank had been a frequent customer, years ago. He had met with a friend often in the afternoons. The other man still came sometimes. She tried to find out more, but he had told her all he knew.

She had to make do with that. If she got the chance, she'd return another time, to see if her father's friend was there.

She asked if she could leave a note. When presented with a small piece of paper, she wrote only she was trying to find out information about Hank Pendarvis and would return in three days.

She dare not at this point mention her tenuous relationship to the sheikh. She did not want anyone trying to reach her at the villa. Until she knew more, she had to keep her secret.

Bethanne returned to the car then instructed the driver to take her to the best store in the city. She wanted to search for the perfect outfit to wear to a polo match. She did not need Rashid buying every stitch she wore.

When Bethanne returned to the villa late in the afternoon, the driver must have had some way to notify Fatima. The older woman met her in the lobby, her face disapproving, her tone annoyed as she said something Bethanne didn't understand. Probably chastising her for leaving her chaperone behind.

To her surprise, Rashid al Harum came from the library.

"Ah, the eternal pastime of women—shopping," he said, studying the two bags with the shop's name on the side.

"Your stores had some fabulous sales," she said. "Wait until you see the dress I bought for the polo match. I hope it's suitable—the saleswoman said it was." Conscious of the servants, she smiled brightly and hurried over to him, opening the bag a bit so he could peek in.

He did so and smiled. Glancing at the staff, he stood aside.

"Perhaps you'd join me in the salon."

"Happy to," she said.

He spoke to Fatima and the woman came to take Bethanne's bags, then retreated.

"Is anything wrong?" Bethanne asked once the two of them were alone in the salon.

"Not at all. I have some spare time and came to see if you wanted to have lunch together. I have not forgotten you wanted to see some of my country. Where did you go this morning?"

"To a place in the old town. I walked around a square there, saw a small market. Then went shopping for the dress."

"I'd be delighted to show you more of the old town, and some of the countryside north of the city, if you'd like."

"Yes. I would. I probably won't get the chance to visit Quishari again after I leave." Especially if she didn't find her father, or convince Rashid he was innocent.

"And I remember you like exploring new places," he commented, studying her for a moment.

"I'll run upstairs and freshen up. I can be ready to leave in ten minutes."

"There's no rush."

She smiled again and dashed up to her room. She should have been better prepared for Rashid, but had not expected him to disregard work to spend time with her. She was delighted, and hoped they'd find mutual interests for conversation. She could, of course, simply stare at him all day—but that would look odd.

Rashid walked to the opened French doors. He gazed out at the gardens, but his thoughts centered on his American visitor. Bethanne fascinated him. Her profession was unusual for a woman. Yet whenever she was around him, she appeared very feminine. He liked looking at her with her fair skin, blue eyes and soft blond hair. Her casual manner could lead some to believe she was flighty—but he'd checked her record and it was spotless. He also found her enthusiasm refreshing after his own rather cynical outlook on life. Was that an American trait? Or her individual personality?

Rashid knew several American businessmen. Had dined with them and their wives over the years. Most of them cultivated the same aloof cosmopolitan air that was so lacking in Bethanne. Maybe it was that difference that had him intrigued.

His mother had called again that morning, bemoaning the fact Bethanne was visiting and that Haile had not come. When he'd told her he was just as well out of the deal, she'd appeared shocked. Questioning him further, she'd become angry when he'd said he wasn't sure the arrangement had been suitable in the long run. He didn't come out and tell her of firm plans with Bethanne, but let her believe there was a possibility.

He almost laughed when his mother had tentatively suggested Bethanne wasn't suitable and he should let her help him find the right bride. He knew he and Bethanne didn't make a suitable pair. Yet, if he thought about it, she would probably have beautiful children. She was young, healthy, obviously intelligent.

He stopped. It sounded as if he were seriously considering a relationship with her. He was not. His family would never overlook what her father had done. And after the aborted affair with Marguerite, he didn't fully trust women. He would do better to focus on finalizing the details of the agreement with al Benqura.

His mother had reminded him she expected a different guest, and so would others.

"Until they see Bethanne. Then they'd know why she's visiting," he'd said, hoping to fob her off. It would certainly give a shot in the arm to the gossip circulating. And, he hoped, throw off any hint of scandal the minister might try to expose. Animosity ran deep between them. Rashid would not give him anything to fuel their feud.

He'd already invited Bethanne to the polo match. Perhaps

a dinner date or two, escorting her to a reception, would give gossips something else to talk about. It would not be a hardship. And al Benqura was in a hurry to finish the deal, as Rashid had suspected. Once the papers were signed, Bethanne would be leaving. Life would return to normal and no one except he and she would know the full circumstances of the charade. The thought was disquieting. Maybe he wouldn't be in so much of a hurry to finalize everything.

Bethanne took care when freshening up. She brushed her hair until it shone. Tying it back so it wouldn't get in her face, she refreshed her makeup. She felt like she was on holiday—lazing around, visiting old town, now seeing more of the country. Spending time with a gorgeous man. What was not to like about Quishari?

She was practical enough to know she wasn't some femme fatale; she'd never wow the sheikh like some Arabian beauty would. Haile had had that sultry look with the fine features, wide chocolate-brown eyes and beautiful dark hair so many Arab women had. Next to them, she felt like a washed-out watercolor.

Leaving her room, she started down the stairs.

"Prompt as ever," he said from the bottom.

She glanced down at him, gripping the banister tightly in startled surprise. She could take in how fabulous he looked in a dark suit, white shirt and blue-and-silver tie. His black hair gleamed beneath the chandelier. His deep brown eyes were fixed on her. Taking a breath, she smiled and tried to glide down the stairs. Was this how Cinderella felt going to the ball? She didn't want midnight to come.

"You look lovely," he said.

Bethanne smiled at him. "Thank you, kind sir."

Once seated in the limo, Rashid gave directions to the driver. Bethanne settled back to enjoy being with him.

"So if I'm to watch a polo match on Saturday, maybe I should learn a bit of the finer points of the game," she said as they pulled away from the villa. "What should I watch for?"

Rashid gave her an overview of the game. Bethanne couldn't wait to see Rashid on one of the horses he spoke about. She knew he'd looked fabulous. She had to remind herself more than once on the ride—sheikhs didn't get involved with women from Galveston, Texas.

When they arrived at the restaurant, Bethanne was impressed. It was on the shore of the Gulf, with tall windows which gave an excellent view to the beautiful water. Their table was next to one of the windows, tinted to keep the glare out, making Bethanne feel as if she were sitting on the sand.

"This is fabulous," she murmured, captivated by the view.

"The food is good, as well," he said, sitting in the chair opposite.

The maître d' placed the menus before them with a flourish.

After one glance, Bethanne closed hers and looked back out the window. "Please order for me. I'm afraid I can't read Arabic."

"Do you like fish?"

"Love it."

"Then I'll order the same filet for us both and you'll see what delicious fish we get from the Gulf."

After their order had been taken, Bethanne looked at him. "Do you ever go snorkeling or scuba diving?"

"From time to time," he said. "Do you?"

She nodded. "It's almost mandatory if one grows up in Galveston. I've had some great vacations in the Florida Keys, snorkeling and exploring the colorful sea floor."

"We will have to try that before you go," he said politely.

She studied him for a moment. "I can go by myself, you

know. You don't have to take time away from your busy work schedule. It's not as if—"

His raised eyebrow had her stopping abruptly.

"What?"

"We do not know who can hear our conversation," he cautioned.

She glanced around. No one appeared to be paying the slightest bit of attention to them, but she knew it would only take a few words to cause the charade to collapse and that would undoubtedly cause Rashid a lot of trouble.

"So how goes the deal?" she asked, leaning a bit closer and lowering her voice.

"We should sign soon, if certain parties don't cause a glitch."

"The father?" she asked, feeling as if she were speaking in code.

"No, he'll come round. It's some of our own internal people who are against the proposed agreement who could still throw a wrench into the works."

"And your mother?"

Rashid leaned closer, covering one of her hands with his, lowering his voice. "My mother has no interest in politics or business. She only wants her sons married. Our personal lives have no interest to anyone, unless it causes a breach between me and al Benqura. That's what we are guarding against."

Bethanne knew to others in the restaurant, it must look as if he were whispering sweet nothings. Her hand tingled with his touch. For a moment she wished she dared turn it over and clasp his. The Quishari culture was more conservative than Americans and overt displays of affection were uncommon in public. Still, he had made the overture.

"Do not be concerned with my mother. She will not cause a problem."

"I wished she liked me," she murmured.

"Why? You'll hardly see her before you leave. She will be at the polo match and perhaps one or two events we attend, but her manners are excellent, as I expect yours to be."

Bethanne bristled. "I do know how to make nice in public," she said.

Amusement danced in his eyes. "I'm sure you do."

Their first course arrived and Bethanne was pleased to end the conversation and concentrate on eating and enjoying the view.

"This is delicious," she said after her first bite. The fish was tender and flavorful. The vegetables were perfect.

He nodded. "I hoped you would like it."

Conversation was sporadic while they ate. Bethanne didn't want to disturb the mellow mood she was in as she enjoyed the food. She glanced at Rashid once in a while, but for the most part kept looking at the sea.

When the sugared walnuts appeared for dessert, she smiled in delight. "I didn't know restaurants served these," she said, taking one and popping it into her mouth.

"I ordered them specially for you," he said.

"You did?" Amazing. She'd never had anyone pay such attention to details and then act on their knowledge. "Thank you very much. I love these."

She savored another then asked, "So what happened to your brother? Did he get the fire out?"

"He did. He heads a company that specializes in putting out oil fires as well as acting as consultants for wells around the world."

"Sounds dangerous."

"Putting out the fires can be, but the rest is consulting work."

"Isn't he part of the family business?"

"He is, but more a silent partner in the day-to-day operations. He prefers not to be stuck in an office, as he puts it."

She studied him, taking another walnut and savoring it as she put it in her mouth. "I don't see you as *stuck* in an office. I expect you love pitting your mind against others."

He smiled slightly. "One way to put it, I suppose. I find it satisfying to make deals to benefit the company. Pitting my wits against others in the field and continuing to expand the company beyond what my father did."

"How did your father die?" It was a bold question, given what she'd learned this morning, but she would never have a better opportunity.

"Heart attack. He was only sixty-three…far too young to die."

"I hope heart problems don't run in your family." Nothing said about what caused it. Maybe the timing was coincidental to the disappearance of her father and the plane. She hoped so. It was bad enough they thought her father a thief. Surely they didn't blame him for the old sheikh's death.

"No. He had rheumatic fever as a child and developed problems from that. The rest of us, including two of his older brothers, are fine."

More than fine, she thought, looking away lest she gave him insight into her thought process. Really, Bethanne, she admonished, you've seen other gorgeous men before. Just not so up close and interested in her—even if it was only pretend.

"Ready to leave? We can take the walnuts with us. I want Teaz to drive us up the coast. There are some beautiful spots along the way. And some ruins from ancient times."

Settled in the luxurious limousine a few moments later, Bethanne knew she could get used to such treatment in no time. And she could gain a bazillion pounds if she kept eating the sweets. Just one or two more and she'd stop. Until later.

Rashid gave a running commentary as they drove along one

of the major highways of Quishari. With the Persian Gulf on the right and huge family estates on the left, there was a sameness that gradually changed as they went farther from the city.

Soon they were surrounded by the desert, stretching from the sea to as far to the west as she could see.

"The ruins are best viewed walking through them," he said when Teaz stopped the car. The place was lonely, sandy and windswept, only outlines of the buildings that had once comprised a thriving village.

"Lonely," Bethanne said, staring west. Nothing but miles of empty land. And the memory of people now gone.

"Once it was a lively trading port. You can see a few of the pilings for the piers in the water. It's estimated these are more than two thousand years old."

"Makes America seem like a toddler. Most of our history goes back four hundred years—once the Europeans settled in. I'd like to see this from the air. Tell me more."

By the time the sun was sinking lower in the sky, they'd gone north almost to the border and turned to head for the villa. Bethanne enjoyed every moment. It was obvious that Rashid loved his country and enjoyed sharing his devotion with his guest. She learned more about the history of the area in their ride than she'd ever learned in school or from her father. Rashid had appeared surprised at the knowledge she did have.

"Tomorrow we can take the plane up again. Fly over the ruins and maybe west. There are a few oases that are large enough to support small communities."

"Did your family gather at the villa for holidays?" she asked.

"For some of them. Other times we met at my father's home. But the family loved the villa. In the summer, my parents often spent several weeks visiting my grandmother and enjoying the sea. My brother and I loved those times."

Rashid escorted her to the door when they arrived.

The butler met them, speaking rapidly to Rashid.

"We seem to have company," Rashid said to her in English. "My brother."

"Oh. Do you want me to go on upstairs?"

"No, come meet Khalid."

When they entered the salon, a man sitting on one of the chairs reading the newspaper rose. For a split second, Bethanne stared. He looked just like Rashid. Twins!

Then he turned to face them and the image was disturbed by the slash of burned skin going from just beneath his right eye, down to the collar of his shirt in a disfiguring swath. Bethanne caught her breath, trying not to imagine the pain and suffering that had resulted from such a burn.

"Bethanne, this is Khalid."

"How do you do. Rashid didn't tell me you two were twins."

Khalid nodded but stayed where he was, his eyes alert and suspicious.

"He told me about your plan to fool the world. Stupid idea," Khalid said.

She blinked at the hostility, then glanced at Rashid, who shrugged. "So you say. If it holds off the wolves until the deal is signed, I'm good with it. What brings you here?"

"I wanted to meet her," Khalid said.

Bethanne walked over and sat down. "Now you have. Questions?" She had spent her fair share dealing with obstreperous officers in the past. And some cranky clients. She could handle this.

"Do not cross the line," Rashid warned his brother.

"What do you expect from this?" Khalid said, ignoring his twin.

"A signed acceptance of the jet aircraft I delivered and a

few days exploring a country I have long wanted to see," Bethanne responded quickly.

Rashid watched his brother ask more questions than he should have. He was looking for a gold digger and that was not Rashid's assessment of Bethanne. She was more concerned with clearing her father's name than getting clothes or money from him. Not that Rashid had any intentions of providing his visitor anything more than was needed to attend the events where he'd show her off. Khalid was worried for naught.

"Did you get that oil fire out?" she asked at a pause in the interrogation.

Khalid nodded. "How do you know about that?"

"My dear friend Rashid tells me everything," she said sweetly.

Rashid laughed aloud. "Subtlety is not your strong suit. Leave her alone. I'm happy with the arrangement we have. No need to look for trouble where there is none."

Khalid studied her. Bethanne met his gaze with a considering one of her own.

"We are dining in this evening—would you care to join us?" Rashid asked.

He decided in that instance to stay for dinner. Maybe a few hours in Bethanne's company would end his brother's suspicions and gain his own cooperation in the situation.

CHAPTER FOUR

PROMPTLY at eight the next morning, Bethanne descended the stairs, dressed in her uniform. She was looking forward to another ride over Quishari. She and Rashid had discussed the trip last night. It would give one of his pilots a chance at the controls. She knew he would love the plane.

And she would spend more hours in Rashid's company. She was treasuring each, knowing the memory of their time would be all she'd have in the future. But for now, she relished every moment.

Fatima sat on one of the elegant chairs in the foyer. She rose when Bethanne reached the tiled floor. Saying something in Arabic, she smiled politely. Bethanne hadn't a clue what she said, but smiled in return.

The limo was in front and whisked them both away. Obviously today was a day that needed a chaperone. Was she going on the plane with them as well?

Bethanne had braided her hair in a single plait down the back to keep it out of the way. Her uniform was a far cry from the silk dresses she'd been wearing. Still, this was business. It would have been highly inappropriate for her to wear one of the dresses when flying the plane.

The jet gleamed in the sunlight when they arrived. Ground

crewmen stood nearby, but no one stood next to the plane. Once she and Fatima got out of the limo, the translator broke away from the group and headed their way.

"His Excellency and Alexes are already in the plane," he said with a slight bow.

Bethanne's heart skipped a beat and then began to race.

"I'll start the ground checklist," she said, ignoring her clamoring need to see Rashid again. She had her tasks to perform to carry everyone safely. "Ask Fatima if she wishes to accompany me or board now?"

A quick interchange, then he said, "She will remain by the stairs until you are ready to enter."

Bethanne took her time checking the aircraft then nodded to Fatima and climbed the steps to the plane. After the bright sunshine, it took a couple of seconds for her eyes to adjust. She saw an older man talking with Rashid in the back of the cabin. Starting back toward them, Bethanne watched as they studied the communication panel.

Rashid saw her and introduced the pilot. "We are looking at the various aspects of the aircraft. This one has more features than the one I've been using."

"But the one that was lost had some of these same capabilities," the pilot murmured, still looking at the dials and knobs.

The plane that was lost—was that the one her father had flown? The pilot was someone who might have known Hank. She hoped they had some time together on today's flight so she could ask him.

"If you are ready to depart, Alexes would like to sit in the cockpit to observe and then fly it once you give the go-ahead."

"I'm sure you'll be ready in no time," she said to the pilot. "For all the technology this baby carries, she's quick to respond and simple to fly."

The man didn't look convinced. Bethanne wondered if he was unsure of her own skills, or those of the plane.

"Fatima will accompany us," Rashid said. He handed Bethanne a topographical map. "I thought we could first fly over the ruins from yesterday, and then head west, toward one of the oases I spoke of."

"Sounds great. Did you already file the flight plan?"

"Alexes did."

"Then let's go."

The pilot bowed slightly to the sheikh and followed Bethanne into the cockpit. He slid into the copilot's seat and began scanning the dials and switches.

Bethanne smoothly taxied and took off, taking the route the pilot had filed with the ground control. She talked to the pilot the entire time about what she was doing and how the plane responded. His English was excellent and he quickly grasped the intricacies of the new jet.

When they reached their cruising altitude, she banked easily and headed north as the flight plan outlined. The sea was sparkling in the sunshine. The shoreline, irregular below them, gleamed. The vegetation edging the beach contrasted with the white sand and blue waters.

Even as she conversed with the other pilot, Bethanne scanned the land below, wondering if her father had flown this exact route. Her recall of the topographical map showed when they turned inland she would be flying almost directly west. Was that a routine flight for the old sheikh?

Rashid al Harum opened the cockpit door and looked in. "What do you think, Alexes?" he asked, resting one hand on the back of Bethanne's seat.

The pilot responded in Arabic and when Rashid spoke in the same language, the man looked abashed.

"My pardon. I told His Excellency that the plane handles like a dream. If I may take over for a while?"

Bethanne nodded and lifted her hands.

"Ahh, it does respond like a dream," Alexes said a moment later, approval in his voice.

"Below are the ruins," Rashid said, looking over her shoulder.

Bethanne looked out of the window, seeing the outlines of the structures they'd viewed yesterday. She kept her eyes on the ground when Alexes banked slightly so she could see the old piers marching out in the water. The crystal clarity of the Persian Gulf enabled her to clearly see each one. Her imagination was sparked by the picture below. Who had lived there? How had their lives been spent? What would they think of people soaring over them in planes they probably never even dreamed about?

Slowly the plane turned and the ruins were behind them. Below was only endless sand with hardy plants which could survive the harsh conditions. The scene became monotonous in the brown hues.

Bethanne looked over her shoulder at the sheikh. "How long to the oasis?" she asked.

"We'll be there in time to have lunch before returning. Once you're reassured Alexes knows what he's doing, perhaps you'd join me in the main compartment. Try out that sofa again."

She nodded, her heart skipping a beat. She didn't need to try out the sofa; she knew it was the height of luxury. She would love to spend a bit more time with Rashid, however. And demonstrate to the other pilot she trusted him with the plane.

The pilot seemed competent. He was murmuring softly, as if in love with the jet. She knew the feeling. It was her favorite model to fly. Still, she didn't leap at the chance to go back to the cabin. She had to focus on her primary responsibility, which was completing delivery of the aircraft—not spending time with the sheikh. She reviewed the various features of the cockpit, quoted fuel ratios, aeronautic facts and figures and answered all Alexes's questions.

When she was satisfied he could handle things, she turned over the controls and rose to head to the back. Fatima was dozing in one of the chairs near the rear.

Rashid looked up from a paper he was reading and watched as she crossed the small space and sat beside him on the long sofa.

"Alexes handling things well?" he asked.

"Of course. He said it was similar to another Starcraft plane he used to fly as backup. What happened to that one?"

"It was the one your father took—they both vanished," he said, putting aside his paper.

"It's hard to hide an airplane."

Just then the plane shuddered and began to dive. Bethanne took a split second to act. She was on her feet and heading for the cockpit when it veered suddenly to the right. She would have slammed into the side if Rashid had not caught her and pulled her along.

Opening the cockpit door a second later, she saw Alexes slumped over the controls. The earth rushed toward them at an alarming rate.

Rashid acted instantly, reaching to draw Alexes back. Bethanne slid into her seat and began to pull the plane from the dive. Rashid struggled to get Alexes out of the seat, but the man was unconscious and a dead weight. He called for Fatima and she hurried forward to help him, trying to guide the unconscious pilot's legs away from the controls as the sheikh pulled him from the copilot's seat. Once clear, she helped the sheikh carry him to the sofa while Bethanne regained control of the plane.

In only seconds the jet had resumed a normal flight pattern and once she verified the altitude, she resumed their approved flight track. Glancing around, she was relieved there were no other planes in sight.

"How is he?" she called back. The door separating the cockpit from the cabin had been propped open.

"Still unconscious…most likely a heart attack," Rashid called, loosening Alexes's collar.

"Oxygen is by the first-aid kit in the galley," she yelled back. She contacted ground control. Citing an emergency, she was directed to the nearest airport, in Quraim Wadi Samil, a few miles to the south of their original route.

Glancing over her shoulder, Bethanne could glimpse most of the cabin. Fatima held the portable oxygen tank while Rashid was still bent over the pilot. She shivered, hoping he was all right. What had happened?

In seconds Alexes's eyes flickered. He spoke in Arabic. Bethanne didn't understand him, but applauded Rashid's calm reply. In moments the sheikh had the older man take some aspirin and elevated his legs and feet. His color was pale, his speech slurred slightly.

"Might be a stroke," he called. "We'll head back immediately."

"They've directed me to an airport in Quraim Wadi Samil. It's closer and an ambulance will be standing by," she responded. She looked back again. "How's he doing?"

"Breathing hard. His color isn't good. How much longer?"

Contacting ground control, she requested emergency clearance for the airport and requested information on flight time remaining.

It came immediately. With new coordinates she altered course. In less than ten minutes she saw the small airport. In another ten, they were on the ground and the requested ambulance was already on its way to the hospital with Alexes. The sheikh conferred with the medical personnel before they left, then turned back to the two women standing at the bottom of the stairs.

"You handled that emergency well," Rashid said, his eyes rested on her.

"I was really scared to death. The plane responded well, however, and here we are. It's what I'm trained to do. What did the emergency medical technician say? Will he be all right?"

"Too early to tell. We'll follow to the hospital and see what we find out." He looked at the older woman and said something to her. She smiled and nodded, happiness shining from her face.

"What did you tell her?" Bethanne asked.

"That she was an asset in saving his life. It was providence that she was here and had Haile not left, things might have turned out differently."

"Helps with her guilt over Haile's defection, I'm sure," Bethanne said.

A cab drove up as he was speaking. The driver stopped near the plane and quickly got out, speaking to Rashid.

"Our transportation," he said.

"That was fast."

"I had one of the medical personnel radio for a cab. It'll take us to the hospital and I can decide our next move after I see how Alexes is doing."

"Will the plane be okay here?" Bethanne asked. They were on the far end of the airport tarmac. There were no personnel around and no fencing or other protection for the plane. Still, it was a small airport and so far off the beaten track, Bethanne couldn't imagine anyone wanting to harm the aircraft.

"It will be fine."

The cab was a standard sedan. Comfortable, but a far cry from the limo she'd been using. Oh, oh, she warned herself, don't be expecting that kind of luxury in the future.

* * *

When they arrived at the hospital, Alexes had already been cleared through the emergency room and was in a private room, with a nurse in constant attendance. Bethanne sat in the waiting room with Fatima while Rashid dealt with the paperwork. When he returned, she stood.

"Is he going to be all right?" she asked.

"Too early to tell, the doctor said." He looked worried. "I called the office to notify his family. If they wish to come here to be with him, I'll arrange for transportation."

Bethanne glanced around at the small facility. "Is this place equipped to deal with his situation?" she asked softly.

"It is not the latest in medical technology, but fortunately the doctors on staff are proficient. He will get good care here. Once he's stabilized, we can fly him back to Alkaahdar."

"And in the meantime?"

"We'll stay. Until we know something for certain."

He spoke to Fatima, who nodded.

"We'll find a hotel and check in. Then lunch. It's past one. Then you two can rest until we learn more about Alexes."

When they met for lunch on the small veranda of the hotel on the square, Bethanne wished she had something to wear besides her uniform. It still looked fresh and would have to do, but the warmth of the day had her wishing for one of the summer dresses in the closet at the villa. Something more feminine than a navy shirt and khaki pants.

Rashid sat at one of the tables. She joined him and he rose as she approached.

"Fatima decided to have lunch in her room. She wishes to lie down afterward," he said as he held the chair for Bethanne. "I think the excitement is catching up with her."

"I hope the situation didn't give her a fear of flying," she said.

"We're safe—that's what counts. I ordered already—a light

lunch since it is so late. We'll eat here tonight if we don't have definite word about Alexes before then."

Bethanne nodded. She hoped the other pilot would recover quickly, and be ready to fly again soon. For a moment she wondered what she'd do if she ever had to stop flying. She loved it so much, it would be a drastic change for her life.

The entire situation spooked her a bit. If Alexes had been flying solo, he could have crashed and no one would likely know why. Is that what happened to her father? A crash in some lonely location that no one had found?

"I hope he's going to be okay." She felt an immediate affinity to the older pilot. She hoped he recovered from whatever hit him and could continue flying.

Once they were served, Rashid asked if her room was to her liking.

"It's clean and neat and overlooks the square. Charming, actually."

"Not like the villa."

"Nice in its own way," she replied. "This changes your plans, doesn't it? You didn't expect to be away from the office all day."

"I can be reached by phone if there is an emergency. The staff is capable of handling things. Shall we explore the town after lunch?"

"I would love to."

When they started out, Rashid insisted on buying her a wide-brimmed hat to shelter her head from the sun.

"You aren't wearing one," she said as they left the gift shop.

"I'm used to the sun. Your skin is much fairer than mine and I don't want it burned."

She smiled, feeling cherished. No one had looked out for her in a long, long time.

They walked around the square, looking into the shops, but

when asked if she wanted to enter any, she declined. She wanted to see as much of the town as she could. The old buildings had ornate decorative carvings and bas-reliefs that intrigued her. The cobblestone streets showed wear but were still functioning centuries after they'd first been laid down.

"Tell me about this place. It's old, feels steeped in history. Is it a true representation of old Quishari?"

Rashid gave her a brief history of the town, telling her it had been on the trade routes, a favorite resting place because of the plentiful water.

As the afternoon grew warmer, she could feel heat radiating from the walls as they passed. Turning a corner and exploring some of the side streets put them in line with the breeze and it was pleasant.

"The air feels drier than the coast," she commented.

"Quite. There's a danger of dehydration. We'll stop soon and have something to drink."

Stopping after three o'clock for cold drinks at a small sidewalk café, she was glad the tables had umbrellas. Even with the hat, she was hot beneath the sun. Yet she relished the sights. She loved the sense of timelessness. This town had been here for a thousand years and would likely be around another thousand. If only the walls could talk.

"Will we be able to walk out on the desert a little?" she asked.

"We can ask the driver to take us as far out as you wish to go."

"Just enough to get the feel for it. It's amazing to me anyone can live in the desert."

"The old tribes knew the water spots which were crucial for survival. Caravans and nomads once roamed known trails. Now the routes are known to fewer and fewer people."

When they returned to the hotel, Rashid summoned the same cab. He spoke with the driver and before she knew it, she was sitting in the backseat with Rashid as the man drove crazily toward the west.

"So we ditch the town and take off," she murmured, feeling the delightful cool air from the air conditioner.

"For a while. It's best to see the desert with those interested, not those who wish they were elsewhere."

She laughed and settled down to enjoy the drive. To the right were rows of oil wells, the steady rising and fall of the pumpjacks timeless.

"I've seen those pumps in California," she commented. "In one place they are even painted to look like whimsical animals," she said, watching the monotonous up-and-down action of the machines.

"These kind of pumps are used all over the world. I had not thought about decorating them. They're functional, that's all."

"Is this an oil field that belongs to your company?"

"It is."

"Do you come here often?"

"No. Only once before, actually." He was silent for a moment, then said softly, "It was my father's special project. The wells don't produce as much as in other areas, but he insisted on keeping the field going, and on checking on it himself. I came with him once. It held special attraction for him, not so much for me. As long as there are no problems, I don't need to visit. Khalid comes occasionally."

"Must be nice for the local economy."

"One reason my father kept it going, I think. The discovery of oil helped revive the town and he felt an obligation to keep it going."

"And you do as well."

He shrugged. "I try. My father was a great man. I'm doing my best to do what I think would make him proud."

"Keep an open mind about mine," she said.

He looked at her, eyes narrowed. "What further is there to discuss?"

"We don't know what happened. But I know my father. And he was an honorable man. He would not have stolen your father's plane."

"My father was also an honorable man. The betrayal of his pilot and the disappearance of the plane caused such stress and anxiety he suffered a heart attack, which killed him. It isn't only the betrayal but the end result I find abhorrent."

Bethanne stared out across the desert as if she could search around and find a clue as to what happened to her father. She had only her belief in her dad to sustain her. "I have faith in my father just as you do in yours," she said slowly.

"It is not something we are going to agree on," he said.

"Tell me about being a twin," she said, turning to look at Rashid. It was a definite change of subject, but she wanted the afternoon to be special—not have them at odds because of the past. "I don't even have a sibling, much less a twin. It is true, you're so close you can read each other's mind?"

"Hardly. I can sense things when we are together—like if he's angry and hiding it. But we are two individuals. Growing up was fun. We delighted in playing tricks on our parents and tutors, switching identities, that sort of thing."

"Tell me," she invited.

He spoke of when he and Khalid were boys, visits to the villa to see their grandmother, trips to Europe and other countries around the Mediterranean Sea.

To Bethanne, it sounded glorious. So different from her childhood in Texas. She laughed at some of the antics he described, and felt a bit of sadness for their homesickness when sent to school in England for eight years when Rashid told her how much they'd missed their country.

When he spoke to the driver, he stopped. Rashid looked at

Bethanne. "When we get out, look in all directions. Nothing but desert."

She did so, stepping away from the car, seeking all she could from her senses. The air was dry, hot. The breeze was soft against her skin, carrying the scent of plants she didn't know. In the distance the land shimmered in heat waves, and she thought she saw water.

"A mirage," she breathed softly.

"There?" Rashid stood next to her at the rear of the cab, bending down so his head was next to hers so he could see what she saw. He pointed to the distant image and she nodded. "It does look like water, but we would never find it."

"I know. I have only seen one other mirage. This is fascinating. And quiet. If we don't speak, I think I can hear my heartbeat in the silence."

He didn't reply and for several long moments Bethanne absorbed everything, from the awesome, stark beauty of the desert to the heat from Rashid's body next to hers, his scent mingling with that on the wind. She never wanted to forget this special moment.

Turning, she was surprised how close he stood. "Thank you for bringing me," she said.

To her surprise, he put his palm beneath her chin and raised her face to his. "You constantly surprise me," he said before kissing her.

His lips were warm against hers, moving slowly as if savoring the touch. He pressed for a response and Bethanne gave it to him, sighing softly and stepping closer. His lips opened hers and his tongue teased her. She responded with her own and was drowned in sensation. Forgotten was the world; she was wrapped up in emotions and feelings and the exquisite touch of his mouth against hers. Only the wind was witness, only the sand reflected the heat of passion.

All too soon he ended the kiss and gazed down at her as she slowly opened her eyes. His dark gaze mesmerized. Her heart pounded, her blood sang through her body. If she could capture only one moment of her entire life to never forget, it would be this one.

"We should head back," he said.

The spell shattered. She stepped back and turned, trying to regain her composure so he would never know how much the kiss meant.

"I'm ready. Thank you for bringing me here. It is a special spot." And would forever remain so.

The drive back to Quraim Wadi Samil was silent. Bethanne hugged the sensation of his kiss to herself as the desert scenery whizzed by. Before long the roof lines of the buildings could be seen. They drew closer by the moment. As she and Rashid drew further apart. It had been a whim, an alignment of circumstances—the scare in the plane, the worry about the pilot, being away from home. It meant nothing beyond they were glad to be alive.

She wished it had meant something.

Dinner that evening was again on the terrace of the small hotel. Fatima joined them and the sheikh kept the conversation neutral, translating back and forth between the two women. Bethanne wasn't sure if she were glad Fatima was present or not. It kept things on an even keel, preventing her from reading more into the afternoon's outing than warranted. But it also meant she had to share the precious time with Rashid. And of course the topic of conversation remained focused on Alexes. The doctor had been cautiously optimistic.

Rashid had obtained the report upon their return to the hotel. It looked as if it was a small stroke.

"But he'll fully recover?" Bethanne asked when Rashid told Fatima.

"That's what the tests are assessing. I hope so. But I don't know if he'll ever fly again."

Bethanne nodded. "Or at least not as a solo pilot," she said. "If he were copilot, there'd be someone else in case of another emergency." Her heart hurt for the man. Flying was a way of life; how sad if it ended prematurely.

Rashid nodded. "However, I do not want my family or employees put in any danger if unnecessary. Alexes has served us well for many years. He will not be abandoned."

Sending up a quick prayer for his recovery, Bethanne asked if he would be released before they returned to Alkaahdar.

"Unlikely. We will return in the morning. He'll need care for several days."

Fatima spoke.

"She wonders when she will return home," Rashid said to Bethanne.

"She doesn't need to stay on my account," she replied.

"I believe my mother is more comfortable with her as your chaperone. Otherwise, you might have to stay with my mother."

Bethanne stared at him in dismay. "You can't be serious."

"If we are to continue the pretense, we need to be authentic. I would not have a woman in a home I owned without a proper chaperone—not if I were serious about making her my wife."

"That's totally old-fashioned."

"We are an old culture. We have certain standards and procedures that have served us well for generations. One is the sacredness of the marriage bond. And the high standards we hold for women we make our wives."

"So you might have a fling with someone in another country, but once in your own, it's old-world values all the way?"

He nodded, amusement showing at her indignation.

"I protect whom I'm interested in. There would be no gossip or scandal. The full authority of the al Harum family would be behind the woman I showed interest in—as it would for Khalid's chosen bride."

"Is he also getting married?"

"Not that I know of. He's not the older son."

Bethanne thought it over for a moment. In an odd way, it was interesting. Old-fashioned and a bit chauvinistic, but romantic at the same time. A woman who truly caught Rashid al Harum's interest and affection would be cherished, cosseted and treated like royalty at every turn.

Lucky girl!

The next morning Bethanne piloted the plane back to Alkaahdar. Rashid sat in the copilot's seat. Alexes had been declared out of danger, but the doctor in charge wanted him to remain a bit longer for observation to assess his reaction to medications. He would be transported home in another company plane in a few days' time.

As she flew back, Bethanne was lost in thought as she studied the landscape, so different viewed from the air than on the ground. There were endless miles of sand beneath them, no signs of life. Yet she'd felt the vibrancy of the desert when they'd stopped yesterday.

In a short time she saw the high-rises of the city on the horizon.

"I can't imagine living down there without the modern conveniences," she said.

"My brother likes the challenge. He goes to the desert a lot. I'm like you. I prefer modern conveniences—especially air-conditioning."

"Funny that twins would be so different."

"More a difference in circumstances. When Khalid was

burned so badly, he withdrew. I know the woman he thought to marry was horrified and did not stand by him. I thought he was better out of that arrangement, but it was still a bitter pill to swallow. It was after that he began seeking solitude in the desert."

"Can't the burned skin be fixed with plastic surgery?"

"He had some operations, decided against any more. He says he's satisfied."

Bethanne knew even with the badly burned slash of skin, Khalid was as dynamic and appealing his brother. "Too bad."

"It could have been worse. He could have died."

Once they landed at the airport, the familiar limousine slid into place near the plane.

"I have work to do. Teaz will take you to the villa. I'll see you for dinner around seven?" Rashid said.

"I'll look forward to it," she said, disappointed they wouldn't spend this day together. "I'll double-check things on the plane before leaving."

Since Rashid would be tied up until later, she'd revisit the café in the square near where her father once lived to see if his friend had shown up. The longer she was around Rashid, the more she wanted to clear her father's name. It grew in importance as her feelings for the sheikh grew.

CHAPTER FIVE

SATURDAY Bethanne rose early. Today was the polo match, followed by a dinner dance in the evening. She hoped the dress she'd brought for the actual match was suitable. The light blue cotton had appealed to her the moment she'd first seen it. It was slightly more casual than the dresses Rashid had bought. Suitable for outdoors and easily cleaned if something spilled on it. She hoped she'd chosen well. The sparkle in her eyes and the blush of color on her cheeks showed how excited she was with the excursion.

The maid knocked on the door before nine and told her Rashid was waiting.

Grabbing her small purse and the wide-brimmed hat Rashid has bought in Quraim Wadi Samil, she hurried down to greet him.

He was waiting in the foyer, dressed in jodhpurs and a white shirt opened at the collar. He watched as she ran lightly down the stairs while she could hardly take her eyes off him. He looked fabulous.

"I'm ready," she said as she stepped onto the tile floor.

"A good trait in a woman, always being on time."

"Comes from pilot training, I expect," she said as they went outside.

A small sports car stood where the limousine normally parked.

"I will drive," Rashid said, escorting her to the passenger's side.

Bethanne loved riding in a convertible—especially beside Rashid.

Within twenty minutes, they had reached the polo field. The bustle of activity reminded Bethanne of horse races in Texas. Lots of people walking around, studying horses, reviewing printed programs, laughing and talking. Clothing varied from designer originals to the jodhpurs and white shirts that Rashid wore. Once in a while she spotted a man in more traditional robes, but for the most part she could be in England or France, or Texas.

Rashid parked near a stable and Bethanne went with him to one of the stalls where a groom already had a beautiful Arabian saddled.

"This is Morning Star," Rashid said with affection, patting the arched neck of the horse. His glossy chestnut coat gleamed. His mane and tail had been brushed until they looked silky soft.

"He's beautiful," she said, reaching out to pet him as well.

"He is one of four I have. Come, we'll look at the rest, all great animals. But Morning Star is the one I ride most often."

Bethanne loved the entire atmosphere of the event. She was introduced to other players. She petted a dozen or more beautiful horses. She watched as the grooms prepared horses for the event.

Khalid was also riding and they visited him shortly before Rashid escorted her to the viewing stands. His welcome wasn't exactly warm, but better than his mother's was likely to be, Bethanne thought.

"My mother is already in the royal box," Rashid said as they began to climb the stairs.

Bethanne's heart dropped. She had not known she'd be spending time with Madame al Harum. It was enough to put a damper on her enthusiasm. Still, with any luck, the woman would be so busy rooting for her sons, she would ignore the unwelcomed woman her one son was entertaining.

There were several guests in the al Harum box, and Rashid made sure everyone was introduced to Bethanne before he left.

"See you later," he said, with a special caress on her cheek.

She played the part of adoring girlfriend and told him to win for her.

Smiling at the others, she took a seat left for her on the front row and focused on the playing field and not the chatter around her. Not that she could understand it. Just before the match began, Madame al Harum sat in the seat next to her.

The game was exciting and Bethanne was glad Rashid had gone over the main points so she had a glimmer of an idea how it was played. Often she saw a blur of horses and riders when the players vied for the ball. Other times Rashid would break free and hit the ball down the field. Or Khalid. His horse was a dark bay. That wasn't the only way she could tell the men apart, but it helped. She seemed tuned in to Rashid and kept her eyes on him for most of the game.

When the match ended, Rashid's team had won by two points. The people in the box cheered and Bethanne joined right in.

"Come, we will meet them for celebration, then return home to change for tonight's fete," Madame al Harum said, touching Bethanne on the shoulder. The older woman walked proudly to the area where the winners were celebrating.

When Rashid saw them, he broke away and crossed swiftly to them, enveloping Bethanne in a hug. She hugged him right back, enthusiasm breaking out.

"It was wonderful! You looked like you were part of the

horse. And that one long drive…I thought the ball would never stop."

"Well done, Rashid," his mother said, watching in disapproval the animation on Bethanne's face.

Khalid came over, hugging his mother and standing with his arm around her shoulders as he greeted Bethanne again.

"Great match," she said with a smile.

He nodded.

"Don't you ever worry you'll get hit by the maillot?"

"It's happened. Glad you enjoyed it. Your first match?" he asked.

"Yes. I hope not my last," she said. Rashid had mimicked his brother with his arm around Bethanne's shoulders. She tried not to be self-conscious, but she knew his mother did not approve. She didn't care. She would not care. It's not as if they'd made a lifelong commitment to each other. The older woman would find out soon enough.

"Come to the dinner tonight," Madame al Harum said to Khalid.

"Not tonight. I have other plans." He gave her a kiss on her cheek, sketched a salute to Rashid and Bethanne and left, weaving his way through the crowd.

His mother watched with sad eyes.

"He never comes," she said.

"Let him find his own way, Mother," Rashid said gently.

After Rashid checked with the groom on the state of his horse, he escorted Bethanne to the sports car.

"So how often do you play? When do you find time to practice? Do you ever have games away from Alkaahdar?" she asked, fascinated by the sport.

He answered her questions as he skillfully drove through

the city traffic, giving Bethanne a fascinating insight to more of his life.

"I'll pick you up at six-thirty," he said when they arrived at the villa. "Dinner starts at seven. And the party will last until late."

"I'll be ready," she said.

Before she could get out of the car, however, he stopped her. "You did well today."

"I will do fine tonight as well," she replied gravely. "I'll be most adoring, now that you won the match."

He laughed at her sassy remark and watched as she entered the house.

Bethanne dressed with care for the dinner. She wore an ivory-white dress from the ones Rashid had bought. The one-shoulder gown fell in a gentle drape down to the floor, moving when she walked, caressing her skin with the softness of pure silk. Minnah came to ask if she could assist and Bethanne asked her to do her hair up in a fancy style.

The quiet woman nodded and set to work when Bethanne sat in front of the vanity.

"Could you also teach me some Arabic?" Bethanne asked.

"Like what?"

"Pleased to meet you. I am enjoying visiting your country. Just a few phrases?"

"It would be my pleasure," the maid said.

For the moments it took the maid to arrange her hair, she also taught Bethanne several phrases. With a skill for mimicking sounds, Bethanne hoped she was getting the correct intonation to the sounds she heard.

Minnah beamed with pleasure a few moments later. Bethanne gazed at herself in the mirror, very pleased with the simple, yet sophisticated style the maid had achieved.

"Thank you," she said in Arabic.

Minnah bowed slightly and smiled. "You pick up the words quickly."

"I'll be repeating them from now until we begin dinner," she said in English.

"His Excellency will be pleased with the effort you have made starting to learn our language. It is good for you to speak Arabic."

Bethanne didn't abuse her of the idea that she was being considered for Rashid's wife. Nothing like servants' gossip to spread like wildfire. That should suit him.

Bethanne was waiting in the salon when Rashid arrived. He wore a tuxedo. She loved the different facets of the man. From suave businessman to casual polo player to elegant sophisticate. She couldn't decide which appealed more.

"Ever prompt," he repeated when he stepped into the salon. "And you look lovely."

"Thank you," she said in Arabic, almost laughing at his look of surprise.

He said several words in that language which had her actually laughing aloud and holding up a hand.

"Please, I only learned a very few—such as please and thank you, nice to meet you and I am enjoying my visit."

"Very well done," he said.

His obvious approval warmed her.

"The dress is lovely, but missing something," he said.

She looked down. "I have a wrap on the chair," she said, moving to gather it.

"I was thinking of jewelry," he said, stepping closer. From his pocket he pulled out a beautiful necklace of sapphires and diamonds on a white gold chain.

Bethanne caught her breath. "It's beautiful." She took a step back. "But I can't wear that. What if it came undone and was lost?" She couldn't replace a fine piece of jewelry like that for years.

"It will not come undone and the stones match your eyes. It will complete the dress."

She looked at the necklace and then at Rashid.

"My intended bride would not come as a pauper to the wedding," he said.

Of course. It was for show. For a moment she was swamped with disappointment. What had she expected—that he'd really give her a lovely piece of jewelry like that?

"Very well, but it's on you if it gets lost."

She stepped forward and held out her hand, but he brushed it aside and reached around her neck to fasten it himself. She stared at his throat, her heart hammering in her chest. The touch of his warm fingers on her neck sent shivers down her spine. She could scarcely breathe.

Bethanne turned when he'd finished, seeking a mirror to see how it looked. There were none in the salon. "I want to see," she said.

"In the foyer, then we should leave."

Standing a moment later in front of the long mirror in the foyer, she gazed at her reflection. She looked totally different. It wasn't only the expensive clothing and jewelry, the sophisticated hairstyle. There was a glow about her, a special look in her eyes. She sought Rashid's in the reflection. He looked at her steadily.

"Thank you. I feel like Cinderella before the ball."

"It does not end at midnight," he said. "Shall we?"

The limo carried them the short distance to the luxury hotel where the dinner was being held. The huge portico accommodated half a dozen cars at a time and Bethanne had a chance to observe the other women getting out of cars and limousines who were wearing designer creations and enough jewelry to open a mega store.

Once inside, Bethanne was delighted with the sparkling chandeliers overhead that threw rainbows of color around the lavish room. Tables were set with starched white linen clothes, ornate silverware and fine crystal glassware. The room was large enough to accommodate hundreds, yet the space was not crowded.

Rashid placed her hand in the crook of his arm, pressing her arm against his side as they walked in. He greeted friends, introducing Bethanne to each. She smiled and gave her newly learned Arabic greeting. Many of the people seemed pleased, and then disappointed she hadn't yet learned more. They encouraged her to continue learning.

An older man stopped their progression. He spoke to Rashid, but his gaze never left Bethanne.

Rashid answered then spoke in English. "Bethanne, may I present Ibrahim ibn Saali, minister of finance for Quishari. He is a great polo fan. I've told him you are my special guest."

"Come to visit Quishari?" the minister asked.

Bethanne smiled brightly. "Indeed, and I'm charmed by what I've seen." She leaned slightly against Rashid, hoping she looked like a woman in love in the minister's eyes.

"I thought another was coming," the minister said.

She looked suitably surprised, then glanced at Rashid. "There had better not be another expected."

He shook his head, his hand covering hers on his arm. "Not in this lifetime," he said. To the minister he nodded once. "We are expected at my mother's table."

"Nice to have met you," Bethanne said in Arabic.

The older man merely nodded and stepped aside.

She could feel his gaze as they crossed to the table.

"He's the one, isn't he?" she asked.

"Indeed. But your acting skills were perfect." He glanced down at her and smiled. "If we keep him satisfied, the deal is as good as done."

When they reached their table, Madame al Harum was already seated. Next to her was an elderly man. He rose when Bethanne arrived and greeted her solemnly. Both expressed surprise at her Arabic response. For a moment she wondered if the older woman would thaw a bit. That thought was short-lived when Madame al Harum virtually ignored Bethanne and indicated that Rashid should sit next to her.

Despite not understanding the language, Bethanne enjoyed herself. The polo club was celebrating their victory and she could clap and cheer with them all. Several speakers were obviously from the club. Rashid leaned closer to give capsulated recaps of the speeches. At one point the speaker on the platform said something that had everyone turning to look at Rashid. He rose and bowed slightly to thunderous applause.

When he sat down and the speaker resumed, she leaned closer.

"What did he say?"

"Just thanks for funding the matches."

"Ah, so you're the sponsor?"

"One of several."

She knew he was wealthy, but to fund a sports team cost serious money. She was so out of her element. No matter how much she was growing attracted to her host, she had to remember in the great scheme of things, she was a lowly employee of a company selling him the jet she'd delivered. He was a wealthy man, gorgeous to boot. He had no need to look to the likes of her when any woman in the world would love to be in her position. How could Haile have chosen someone else over Rashid?

* * *

When the after-dinner speeches were finally finished, a small musical ensemble set up and began playing dance music. Some of the older guests gathered their things to leave, but the younger ones began to drift to the dance floor.

Rashid held out his hand to Bethanne. "Will you dance with me?" he asked.

She nodded and rose.

He was conscious of the stares and some of the conversation that erupted when they reached the dance floor. Her blond hair and blue eyes stood out in this group of mostly dark-haired women. He enjoyed taking her into his arms for the slow dance. She was taller than most women he had dated and it was a novelty to not have to lean over to hear if she spoke. Or to kiss her.

He'd thought a lot about that kiss in Quraim Wadi Samil as they moved with the music. He tightened his hold slightly in remembrance. One kiss had him fantasizing days afterward. He'd kissed his share of women. He'd even thought he loved Marguerite. But Bethanne had him in a quandary. He knew this was an interlude that would end as soon as the contract with al Benqura was signed. Yet he found reasons to seek her out and spend time with her. He loved to hear her talk. She wasn't one to mince words, or be totally agreeable. He knew too many people who sought favor above friendship.

And while he tried to ignore the physical attraction, he couldn't do it. He longed to press her against him, kiss her, make love to her. Her skin was as soft as down. Her sparkling eyes held wit and humor and made him think of the blue of the Gulf on a sunny day. He wanted to thread his fingers through that silky blond hair and stroke it, feeling the softness, the warmth from Bethanne.

Comparing her to other women was unfair—to others. Unlike Marguerite, she was unpretentious and genuine. She did not show an innate desire to garner as much money as she could in a short time. He detected no subterfuge; had heard no hints about keeping the necklace she wore. He smiled slightly when he thought of her worry if it came undone. He would never expect her to repay the cost of the jewelry. When he'd asked his assistant to find something with blue stones, an array had been brought to the office. These sapphires had matched her eyes. He'd chosen it immediately.

How had he known they would match her eyes? He could not even remember what color Marguerite's eyes were. Glancing down, he studied his partner as they circled the room. She looked enchanted. And enchanting. Her gaze skimmed around the room, a slight smile showing her enjoyment. As if she could feel his attention, she looked up.

The blue startled him with its intensity. Her smile made him want to slip away from the crowd to a private place and kiss her again.

"Enjoying yourself?" he said, to hear her speak.

"Very much. This is even better than my senior prom, which was the last formal dance I attended, I think. Some of the gowns are spectacular. I'm trying to remember everything so I never forget."

"There will be others," he said, taking for granted the setting and the people—many of whom he'd known all his life. His polo team members had been friends for years.

"For you. Once you sign that contract, I'm heading back to Texas."

"Or you could stay a little longer," he suggested, wishing to find a way to keep her longer.

From the jump she gave, he'd surprised her with his suggestion.

"I may delay signing the papers until well after the deal is finalized," he said, half in jest. Far from being angry at Haile, he now thanked her for her defection. Otherwise he would not have known Bethanne. What a shame if he'd merely thanked her for delivering the jet and never seen her again.

"Now why would you do that?" she asked, leaning back a bit to smile up at him with a saucy grin.

It took all of Rashid's willpower to resist the temptation to kiss her right there on the ballroom floor. She was flirting with him. It had been years since someone had done that in fun. He knew she had no ulterior motives.

"Alexes might never fly again. Perhaps you could become my personal pilot." He hadn't thought about that before, but it would be a perfect solution. She'd remain in Quishari and he could see her whenever he wanted.

"My home is in Texas," she said slowly. "I don't speak the language here. I have family and friends in Galveston. I don't think it would work."

At least she sounded regretful.

"Think about it before deciding," he said.

"Would there be more dances like this?" she teased.

He laughed and spun her around. "Yes, as many as you wish to attend. I don't go often, except the ones with the polo team. But that could change. I receive dozens of invitations."

"I would imagine attending them all would prove tiring. And it would dim some of the splendor if you saw this kind of thing all the time. What makes it special is being rare."

"A wise woman."

The music ended. In a moment another song began. Rashid held her hand during the short break, rubbing his thumb lightly over the soft skin. The couple next to them smiled but said nothing, for which he was grateful. Even more grateful when the music began again and he could draw her back into his arms again. It had been a long time since he'd enjoyed spending time with anyone beyond his family.

The evening flew by. Bethanne focused on the offhand invitation to stay. She wasn't sure if he were serious or not. It was tempting. Maybe too much of a good thing. What would happen if she actually fell in love with the sheikh and he only wanted her as a pilot because Alexes was incapacitated? She gazed off, picturing him with other women—beautiful women with pots of money. He'd ask her to fly them to Cairo or even Rome on holiday. She'd be dutiful and resentful. She didn't want to fly him and some other woman anywhere. She wanted him for herself.

Startled at her thoughts, she glanced at him quickly, and found his gaze fixed on hers.

"If you are ready to leave, we can return to the villa," he said.

"I've had a lovely time, but it is getting late." Her heart pounded with the newly admitted discovery. She was in love with Rashid.

"Too late for a walk along the beach?"

To walk along the Persian Gulf in the moonlight—who could pass up such an opportunity?

"Never too late for that."

On the ride to the villa, he continued to hold her hand. Bethanne told herself it was merely a continuation of the evening. But she felt special. Would it ever be possible for a sheikh to fall for a woman from Texas? With no special attributes except the ability to fly planes? Undoubtedly when he chose a bride, he'd want a sophisticated woman who was as at home in the capital city as she would be anywhere in the world.

When they reached the villa, he helped her from the limo then bypassed the front door to head for the gardens. The pathways were discreetly lighted by soft lamps at foot level. Selective spotlights shone on a few of the topiary plants; the ambient glow felt magical. Fragrances blended delightfully with the salty tang of the sea. She heard the wavelets as they walked along.

"Should we change?" she asked, concerned for the lovely gown.

"More fun this way."

An unexpected side of Rashid. Every time she thought she had a grasp on his personality, he surprised her.

When they reached the beach, they sat on the chairs to take off their shoes. Rashid rolled his pant legs up and held out his hand for her when she rose. They ran to the water. Bethanne pulled her skirt to above her knees in an attempt to keep the beautiful silk from getting wet, holding it with one hand.

The water was warm. The moon was low on the horizon, painting a strip of white on the calm sea. Stars sprinkled the dark skies. In the distance a soft glow showed where the capital city lay. As if in one accord, they turned and began walking north.

"I can't believe you live in the city when you have this house," Bethanne said. "I'd walk along the beach every chance I got if I lived here."

"You seem to like simple pleasures," he said. Unlike other women he knew who loved new clothes, jewelry and being seen in all the right places.

"What's better? Maybe flying."

"Tell me why you like that so much."

"I'm not sure I can put it into words. There's a special feeling soaring high into the sky. The power of the plane at my command. The view of the earth, seeing the curvature, seeing the land as it is and not as man has rearranged it. I never tire of it."

"I see flying as an expedient way to get from one place to another in the shortest time."

"Then you need to fly in the cockpit more and give work a rest."

He laughed. "I would not be where I am today if I didn't pay attention to business."

"There's such a thing as balance."

"So you suggest I take more time off?"

"Take time to relax. Even in your time off you're busy. Do you ever just lie on the beach and listen to the waves?"

"No."

She danced in the water. "I do when I'm home. Galveston has some beautiful beaches and I like to just veg out and do nothing but stare at the water and let the rhythm of the surf relax me."

"Not often, I bet." She was too full of energy to be content to sit and do nothing for long.

"I guess not. That's why when I do, it's special."

He stopped and turned to face her. "You're special, Bethanne Sanders." He put his free hand around the back of her neck and drew her slowly closer, leaning over to kiss her.

The night was magical, the setting perfection, the woman with him fascinating and intriguing. The temporary nature gave an urgency to their time together. Too short to waste.

She kissed him back, slinging one arm around his neck, her other hand still holding her skirt.

For a long time Rashid forgot about responsibilities, about duties and about the pretense of their relationship. There was only Bethanne and the feel of her in his arms.

Both were breathing hard when he ended the kiss. They were alone on the beach, quite a distance from the villa. He was tempted to sweep her in his arms and find a secluded spot and make love all night long.

"We should return," he said. Duty over desire, hard to harness.

"Yes." She let go of his hand, gathered her skirt in both hands and began walking briskly back to the villa.

"Wait." He hurried to catch her. "Are you okay?" He tried to examine her expression in the faint light but she kept her head averted.

"I'm fine." She did not stop walking.

"Then the kiss upset you."

She stopped at that and turned to glare at him. "It did not upset me. What upsets me is that I don't know the rules of this game. We're pretending. But that kiss seemed real. You are solicitous in public playing the perfect gentleman who is showing someone around. It's all fake. Why the kisses?"

Rashid paused. "Because I can't resist," he answered, daring to reveal his feelings. It had been a long time since he'd let emotion make inroads. Would he regret the confession?

She blinked at that. "What?" It almost squeaked out.

"Why should that surprise you? I find you beautiful, fun, interesting, different. I want to be with you, touch you." He reached out his hand and trailed his fingertips down her bare arm, struck again by the warm softness of her skin. "I want to kiss you."

He could see her indecision. Finally she nodded once. "Okay, but unless we are really going somewhere with this relationship, no more than kisses."

Her words jerked him from the reverie he had of the two of them spending time together. He was not going anywhere with any relationship. He had tried love and failed. He had tried arranged marriage—and that didn't look like it was in the cards, either. Was it too much to ask just to enjoy being together for a while—as long as they both wanted?

"Then I'll just have to settle for kisses," he said, drawing her back into his embrace.

Bethanne awoke the next morning feeling grumpy and tired when Minnah entered with the usual breakfast fare. She refused to let her crankiness show and almost screamed with impatience while the maid fussed around before leaving. Bethanne had not had a good night's sleep and it was all Rashid's fault. She'd been a long time falling asleep thinking of the kisses at the beach. And the words he had not spoken—that their relationship had a future. That hurt the most.

She sipped her chocolate and wondered what she was doing. Always one to face facts, she simply could not let herself imagine she was falling for the sheikh. She needed to visit the places she wanted to, search for her father and remind herself constantly that Rashid's interests did not coincide with hers.

If she told herself a dozen times an hour, maybe she'd listen. But her heart beat faster just thinking of Rashid and the kisses they'd stolen in the night. His scent was permanently affixed in her mind, his dark eyes so compelling when he looked directly at her she could feel herself returning his regard, wishing there were only the two of them. She had run her hands through his hair, pulled him close and shown her feelings while all he had wanted were a few kisses.

She frowned. Time to rise above the attraction that seemed to grow by leaps and bounds and forget any flighty feelings of love. She had her own quest that being here afforded. Today she'd return to the square to see if the man her father had met had returned. Yesterday the waiter who had spoken to her that first day wasn't there. The one working had not understood English. Maybe the other would be back today.

She'd focus on her search for her father and get over Rashid before she saw him again!

Arriving at the square around ten, she went straight to the sidewalk café, searching for the waiter she'd spoken with before. Thankfully he was there. He came out of the interior to greet her.

"I have a note for you," he said with great pride. With a flourish, he withdrew it from his apron pocket and handed it to her. "I knew you would return," he said.

"Thank you. I'll sit over here and have coffee, please." She sat down at a side table and opened the folded paper.

"Hank was a friend of mine. A fellow American. I will stop by the café each day this week in hopes of seeing you." It was signed, Walt Hampstead.

Another American. That made it simple; at least she and he would speak the same language. She would have needed Teaz to translate if Hank's friend had been a native of Quishari.

"What time did the man come?" she asked the waiter when he delivered her coffee.

"Before lunch each day. He will be here soon." Setting the small cup and carafe on the table, he walked away.

Bethanne sipped the hot beverage while she waited until Walt showed up. She had a feeling things were speeding up and she needed to get any information she could before it was too late.

Sometime later a middle-aged man stopped at her table. She'd been writing a letter to a friend at home and looked up when he cast a shadow over the paper.

"Are you Hank's friend?" he asked. "No, that's not right. You're his daughter, Bethanne."

"Walt?" she asked, feeling emotion welling up inside her.

He nodded. Pulling out another chair, he sat down at the table. "He spoke of you often. I saw a picture once. You were younger. I'm Walt Hampstead. Pleased to finally meet you."

"You knew my father? He mentioned a professor at the university, but not by name. Is that you?"

He nodded. The waiter appeared and Walt gave an order for coffee.

"What happened to him? He's dead, isn't he?" Bethanne asked, hoping Walt would deny it all and tell her where Hank was.

But Walt nodded sadly. "I'm afraid so. I haven't heard from him in almost three years. He was a good friend. Not many Americans live in Alkaahdar. We'd meet and hash over how things were going at home. Expats sharing tales of home to fend off homesickness. And he'd tell me the amazing stories about his daughter."

"Have you lived here long?" Bethanne asked, trying to remember all she'd read and heard about his professor friend. She knew her father had liked the man, but always called him the prof.

"Yes, actually, longer than Hank. I teach English as a foreign language at one of the universities. I married a Quishari woman and we have made our home here."

"Tell me what you know about my father. It's been years since I've heard from him. Time just got away. I've been busy and I thought he was as well. But I can only find out the al Harum family thinks he stole a plane. He wouldn't have!"

The waiter returned with Walt's coffee. Once he'd left, Walt began to speak. "He told me two days before he left that he had a top-secret assignment, then laughed. Just like the movies, he said. I asked him what he was talking about, but he said he was sworn to secrecy, but maybe he'd give me some hints when he returned. He seemed in high spirits and I thought I'd hear from him soon after that. Only I never saw him again."

"I've heard he stole a plane and then vanished," Bethanne said, disheartened. This man had known and liked her father, but knew no more than she did on what had happened to him.

"There were stories going around. Then the head of Bashiri Oil died unexpectedly and the news was full of that and the stories of his twin sons. I never knew the official result of that secret mission," Walt said. He looked pensive for a moment. "Hank was a true friend. It was good to have someone from home to talk over things with. I miss him."

He sipped his coffee. "He flew the plane for the old sheikh, and often told me about where they went, what the different cities were like. Hank loved seeing the world and knew the job he had was great for that. He flew the sheikh to Europe, Egypt, even once to India. Most of the flights were around the Persian Gulf, though."

"Did the secret mission have something to do with the sheikh?"

"That I don't know. I could speculate it was because he worked almost exclusively for the man. But being a secret, I never heard any more. Your father did not steal a plane. He was too honorable for that."

Bethanne felt a wave of gratitude toward Walt for his comment. "I want to find out exactly what happened and let others know he wouldn't do such a thing." Especially let Rashid know. Every time he looked at her he had to remember his belief her father had caused the death of his. It was so unfair!

"Don't know how you'll find out. Do you speak the language?" he asked.

"No, except for pleased to meet you."

"This country is still very much a man's world. I bet they were surprised to discover you're a pilot," he said.

"At first. What happened to my dad's things?" she asked.

"I don't know. I went by his apartment once I realized he was probably dead. It had already been rented and the young woman who answered the door said it had been immaculately cleaned before she moved in. I guess the sheikh's people packed up. I don't know if they threw his things away or stored them."

"My mother tried to find out what happened to him—as his onetime wife. But no one told her anything. I guess if they had any of his things, they would have sent them to her." Bethanne gazed across the square, seeing the buildings her father would have seen every day. She missed him with a tangible pain.

"He spoke of you a lot. You were a bright spot in his life.

He talked about when you'd come to visit and what you two would see."

"We discussed it more than once. I longed to see Quishari, but not like this. It's a beautiful country and I've enjoyed everything I've seen. But I had hoped to see it with my dad."

Walt scribbled on a page of his notebook and tore it out. "Here's my phone number and address. Call me if you need anything. Or wish to visit. My wife would be delighted to meet you. She liked Hank, too. He came to dinner occasionally. Her English is not as fluent as it could be, so she enjoyed listening to our conversations and hearing English spoken by natives."

"Thank you." She took the paper and put it in her purse. "I don't know how you could contact me if you remember anything. I am staying at the sea villa of Sheikh Rashid al Harum. But I have no idea what the address is, or the phone number."

"Do you like him? Hank really respected his father."

"I do like him." Understatement, she thought. But she certainly didn't know this man well enough to even hint at more.

Walt rose. "I'll contact the sheikh if I think of anything else you might wish to know. Nice to have met Hank's daughter. He'd be proud of you. Do consider coming to meet my wife."

Bethanne rose as well and shook hands. "Thanks for coming each day until I was here."

Walt walked away, then stopped and turned. "I do have a photograph of him with me at home. Call me when you can come again and I'll bring it for you to see."

Bethanne nodded. Disappointment filled her and she smiled, blinking away tears. She had so hoped her father's friend would know more. What could a secret mission have been? One filled with danger that ended up costing him his life? How could the old sheikh have demanded that? Did Rashid know?

CHAPTER SIX

BETHANNE rode back to the villa wondering how she could find out more about that secret mission. The only one who had probably known was the old sheikh and he was dead. Would his wife have known anything? If she had, Bethanne would be the last person she'd tell.

Yet everyone seemed to think the plane was stolen. Even so, Hank would have had to file a flight plan. Someone must have known something more about the plane. But she wasn't sure if it were even possible to get a copy in Quishari, much less at this late date.

She could ask Rashid.

Mulling over the possibility of being rebuffed, she weighed it with the possibility of annoying Rashid. But she hadn't a clue where else to go.

When she reached the villa, Fatima was in the foyer, her suitcase beside her. Minnah was there as well and smiled when she saw Bethanne.

"Fatima leaves for the airport. She is returning home," the maid said in English.

Bethanne nodded. "Please tell her I'm sorry for the inconvenience of remaining here when she must have wished to return home immediately."

Minnah relayed the comment, then listened to a rapid burst of speech from Fatima.

"It is she who is grateful for you and whatever arrangement you made with the sheikh that she does not fear returning home. Her charge put her in a very awkward situation and if not for the compassion of the sheikh, she'd not wish to return home. She spoke with her family and there is no retribution awaiting."

"I should hope not," Bethanne said. "She couldn't help—" She paused. Hopefully Fatima had been circumspect in her complaints. Remembering the charade, she finished. "She couldn't help the situation. Tell her I wish her a pleasant journey home."

Once Fatima left, Bethanne went into the library again, wandering around, studying the various books on the shelves. She stopped at the desk and looked at the computer, considering. Turning it on, she sat down and began to search the Internet on any information she could get about Quishari and flight plans and Rashid's father.

Losing track of time, she was surprised when Minnah knocked on the opened door. "Miss, you haven't come for lunch. It is on the terrace. Are you not hungry?"

Bethanne nodded, reluctant to leave her search, but suddenly feeling ravenous.

She was glad she took the break a few moments later when Rashid arrived. She felt almost guilty using the computer to find out more about his father. If her need hadn't been so strong, she would not have done more than a cursory look to learn a bit more about him. Rashid loved his father and wanted to be like him.

She loved her father, and wanted to clear his name.

"Late lunch," Rashid said, drawing out a chair and sitting at the small table.

"I had coffee at a square in the old town midmorning, so wasn't ready to eat until now," she explained. "What are you doing here? Is the workday over?" She knew he devoted many hours to business; was something special going on to have him leave so early?

"I thought we could take the jet up again, fly over the wells to the south and see how things are going. Khalid said the well that was burning has been capped. I'd still like to see how much damage was done. There's an airport nearby and I'll have a car waiting so we can drive to the docks, and then go to the derricks themselves."

"I'm at your command," she said, taking another drink of the iced lemonade she enjoyed so much. This was unexpected, but she relished a chance to see more of what he dealt with daily. She was soaking up as much as she could about Rashid. Down the years, she'd have plenty of memories.

"No rush. Finish your lunch. Where in old town did you go?" he asked.

Bethanne looked at her salad, hoping hearing about her morning wouldn't make him angry. "I went for coffee at the square near where my dad lived. I met another American—a friend of Hank's," she said.

"Anyone I know?" he asked.

"A professor of English at the university. Walt Hampstead. He was pleased to see me. My dad had spoken of me to him. He said he's lived here for more than twenty years. Even married a local girl and they have two children."

Rashid appeared unconcerned by the revelation. "Did you visit the shops?"

"No, I enjoyed the architecture and got a feel for the place. The older section really draws me. I love it. If we are going soon, I'll run up and change."

When they reached the airport an hour later, Bethanne went to the air traffic control office to file a flight plan. The service was quick. As she was turning to leave, she asked if there were archived flight plans for the past five years. The clerk was instantly curious as to why she wanted to know. She shrugged it off as mere curiosity and left. The reports would be in Arabic undoubtedly. No help there—unless Walt could translate them for her.

Rashid had remained with the plane and she did her visual inspection before boarding. He was already in the cockpit and for a moment, the intensity of her wish that things had been different floored her. What would it have been like if she and he had met under different circumstances? If he did not think her father a thief and he was seriously interested in her? That they were going off for a day of fun, just the two of them.

She couldn't help her own excitement at seeing him. Try as she might, it was difficult to remember it was all a charade. Especially after his kisses.

Once soaring over the Persian Gulf, she leveled out the plane and watched the earth below. There were large container ships on the sea, white beaches lining the shore. As they approached the oil rigs several hundred yards offshore, she circled slowly. The fire was out. There was a huge oil tanker anchored on the seaward side of one of the high platforms.

"Taking in oil?" she asked, pointing to the ship.

"Yes. Then it goes to a refinery. That's one of our ships. Another branch of the company," Rashid said. "My uncle runs that. Set us down and we'll head out to the rigs."

They landed on the runway that ran beside the sea. After Bethanne taxied the plane to a sheltered area as directed, she shut down the engines. A dark car drove over and a man jumped out of the driver's side. In only moments they were driving toward the docks.

The launch that took them to the rigs was small and rode low on the water. Bethanne studied the huge platforms that rose on pilings from the sea floor. When they arrived, they had to climb a hundred steps to get to the main platform. The noise surprised her as machinery hummed and clanked as it pumped the crude from beneath the sea.

Khalid was there and strode over to greet them. His manner was reserved and more formal than Rashid's. A difference in the twins. Even though they looked alike, they didn't behave alike.

A moment later Rashid excused himself, saying he had to confer with Khalid on a private matter.

Bethanne walked away, toward the activity near the ship. There were lots of men working in a choreographed way that showed they all knew their respective jobs well.

After watching for a while, she saw a man walk over to say something to her.

"Sorry, I only speak English," she said.

"I speak it," he replied with a heavy accent. "You fly jet that landed at airport?"

"Yes," she replied.

"I used to work planes for the old sheikh." He shrugged. "After he die, I come to oil—" He gestured around them. "Sheikh Rashid don't travel like father did."

"The old sheikh traveled a lot?" she asked, suddenly wondering if this man had known her father.

"More than son." He looked at the activity, studying it a moment as if assessing the efficiency.

"Did you know Hank Pendarvis?" she asked.

He looked back at her and nodded.

"Someone asked me to look him up if I got to Quishari. I think maybe he died several years ago."

The man nodded. "Bad time. Caused old sheikh's death."

"What happened?"

"Flight in west, something special." He paused a moment as if searching for the English word. "Sandstorm crash plane. All die."

"I heard he stole the plane, took an illegal flight." Her heart pounded. This man said her father had crashed. She knew something kept him from contacting her. Still, maybe all hadn't died. Maybe it was even a different plane.

"No. Job for old sheikh."

Bethanne's interest became intense. "Did you tell anyone? Why does everyone believe he stole a plane?"

"Those need to know do."

"Where did he crash?"

"West."

"Who knows about this?"

He shrugged.

Either he knew no more or wasn't going to give her specifics.

"And he is buried out west, too?"

He shrugged. He peered at her closely, searching her face and eyes. "In a town called Quraim Wadi Samil."

Bethanne gave an involuntary start of surprise. "We were just there," she said.

The man shrugged. "Perhaps you go again."

"Why didn't you tell someone at the time? Sheikh al Harum believes he stole the plane."

"No, I tell the sheikh." He looked at where Rashid stood talking with the other men.

A helicopter approached, its blades whipping the air around the platform. It set down near the far edge.

Someone on the platform called the man and he waved. "I go." He loped across the platform and climbed aboard the helicopter with two other workers.

Bethanne stared at the helicopter until it was out of sight. It had not remained on the rig for more than a few minutes. Where was it taking the maintenance worker? She had to have answers. According to him, he had told Rashid.

That didn't make sense. If Rashid knew, why not tell her? He didn't pull punches accusing her father of being a thief, why not say if he were dead? If Rashid knew about the sandstorm and the plane crash, why not tell her?

"Makes you wonder, doesn't it?" a male voice asked to her right.

Turning, she saw Khalid had joined her, staring at the damaged oil rig.

"What?"

"Why men put themselves in danger just to pump oil from beneath the sea," he said.

"Was anyone injured in the fire?"

"One man was killed. Another burned."

"I'm sorry."

"As were we. Mohammad was a good man."

"You were burned once, yet you still fight the fires."

"I do not want fire to win. Why are you here?"

"Rashid brought me."

"I mean, why still in Quishari. You delivered the plane. You did not deliver Haile. Yet you stay."

"Ask your brother."

"I did. He said to stop rumors flying that would damage the negotiations with Benqura. I say forget it. Rashid has little to offer for you to stay—unless you hope to cash in somewhere down the line. A story for a tabloid? A bit of blackmail for your silence?"

She turned to him, affronted at his comment. "I have no intentions of blackmail or talking to a tabloid. Maybe I feel a bit responsible I didn't make sure Haile was on board when we took off. What's not to like about a few days in this lovely country? The villa is exquisite. The staff makes me welcomed. Your brother has shown me places I would not otherwise have seen. I would not repay such hospitality with anything you suggest. I stay because he asked me to." She wasn't going to dwell on the attraction she felt any time she was near Rashid. That was her secret alone.

Khalid studied her for a moment, his eyes assessing. "Maybe. But I don't buy it. Not from an American woman in this day. There has to be something for you in it."

"You're cynical. Maybe I'm enjoying a mini vacation."

"Yet you still fly."

She laughed. "That's for fun."

Rashid walked over. "Khalid." He acknowledged his brother. Rashid looked at Bethanne and then Khalid. "Problems?"

"Just questioning your guest as to why she's here. Watch your back, brother."

"I know what I'm doing," Rashid said with a steely note.

"Maybe it's time for me to leave," she said.

Rashid shook his head, his gaze still locked with his brother. "No one helps out a stranger by pretending so much without something in return," Khalid warned.

Obviously Rashid had not shared all he knew about Bethanne to Khalid. She wanted to confront him about the information she'd learned from the older man. But not with Khalid standing there. How soon could she get back to Quraim Wadi Samil?

Rashid reached out to take her hand, pulling her closer to his side. "Give me an update on the estimated repair time, if you would. Then we'll be going." He was making a definite statement for his twin.

Khalid shrugged and began speaking in rapid Arabic. Bethanne could feel the tension from Rashid as his hand held hers. She let her mind wander since she couldn't understand a word. Why had Rashid asked her to stay—actually almost coerced her? The longer she knew him, the more attached she became. For a few moments, she'd let herself imagine he'd fall in love with her. He'd be as attracted to her as she was to him. Which could lead to happiness beyond belief.

But the reality was more like heartache the size of Texas. She wondered if she dare hint that her feelings were engaged. He'd given her no indication he wanted anything more than a buffer with the minister to buy him some time. And he had not told her the truth about her father.

Yet those kisses had been magical. Had he felt any of the pull she had? With all the women he could date with a snap of his fingers, the fact he spent so much time with her had to mean more than just subterfuge for the minister's sake. Or not. He was so focused on work.

"Is there anything else you wish to see?" Rashid asked her. Bethanne looked at him. Khalid was already some distance away, walking to a group of men near one of the large machines.

"A quick tour would be great. I'll probably never be on an oil rig again." Chafing with impatience to find out more about her father, she refrained from asking him while others could hear. And a quick tour might give her time to figure out how to formulate her question so he'd answer.

"I thought Hasid might have explained some things to you."

"Who?"

"The man you spoke with earlier."

"No." So much for waiting. "Rashid—he said my father's plane crashed near Quraim Wadi Samil. He said you knew."

Rashid stared at her, glancing briefly to the sky where the helicopter had flown. "I do not know what happened to your father. Why would he say that? He never told me. Why does he think that?"

She stared back. Had the other man lied? Why would he? Yet, she couldn't believe Rashid would lie about it. It didn't make sense.

"I'll speak to him. Maybe you misunderstood him. While he speaks some English, he is not fluent. He would have come forward when the plane was lost if he knew anything."

"He says he spoke to you."

"He did not."

She broke her gaze and looked across the water. What to believe? She wished she could return to Quraim Wadi Samil and search for the grave herself. What if he was there? Who could she trust? Who to believe?

The flight home was conducted in almost total silence. Bethanne was trying to figure out how to find out for sure if her father had crashed. Rashid seemed to have dismissed the other man's revelation without a care. Would he if it were true?

Or would he try to stop her if she suggested another visit to Quraim Wadi Samil?

After lunch at the villa, Rashid invited her to go swimming. Bethanne's first response was a yes! She'd love to spend more time with him. But the situation with her father loomed between them.

"I'd like that. I'd also like to learn more about my father."

"Very well. Today we swim. I'll have someone contact Hasid and ask for details. I think you misunderstood him. We have no knowledge of where your father is, or the plane. Do you think a plane crash could be hidden?"

Put that way, she doubted it possible. Still, she had understood what the man said. There was no denying he said he spoke to Rashid.

There was nothing more to be done today. If she didn't get a satisfactory answer from Rashid's questioning, she'd see if she could get back to the oil rig and speak with him again.

* * *

The small boat Rashid drove to was larger than a runabout yet easily handled by one. The marina not far from the villa, it didn't take long to be on their way.

Once out on the water, Bethanne seated in the seat next to his, he turned south. The homes along the shore were varied, from tall and austere, to low with lush gardens and fountains sparkling in the sunlight. Some were set back from the water, some bordered the beach. The farther south they went, the more space grew between homes. Finally he nodded to the thick foliage. "Can you see the villa?"

She caught a glimpse of the roof and a tiny corner of the veranda.

"That's where we eat," she said. It looked smaller from this vantage point. She sighed in pleasure. "It's as pretty from the water as the view is from balcony."

"My grandmother loved beautiful things. This is only one of her homes. They all had gardens that gave her such pleasure."

"My grandmother loves roses. She's a longtime member of the rose society in Galveston and wins prizes for her blossoms year after year."

"Yet another thing we have in common," Rashid said, cutting the engine and letting the boat drift. "Care to swim?"

"I'd love it." She quickly shed the cover-up and reached into the pocket for a band to hold her hair back. Tying it into a ponytail, she waited while Rashid went into the small cabin to change. "Ready when you are," she called.

Rashid stepped out a moment later, clad only in swim trunks. Bethanne almost caught her breath at the masculine beauty. His shoulders were broad; that she already knew. His chest was muscular and toned, not a spare ounce of flesh anywhere. His skin was bronzed by the sun. Masculine perfection. She could sit and stare at the man for hours.

She just hoped she didn't look liked a stunned star-struck groupie. Get your mind on swimming and nothing else, she admonished herself.

Rashid tossed two towels on one of the seats and brought a small ladder from one of the storage compartments. Hooking it to the side, he stood aside, gesturing with one hand.

"After you."

She took a breath, passed close enough to feel the radiant heat from his body, before taking a quick vault over the side. The water closed over her head a moment later, cooling her off in an instant. She felt the percussion of his hitting the water, then rose, blinking in the bright sunshine.

"It's heavenly," she said, turning to swim slowly parallel to the beach. She didn't want to get too far from the boat. The water felt like soft silk against her skin. Its temperature enough to cool, yet warm enough to caress. After a few minutes of swimming, Bethanne stopped and began to tread water. Rashid was right beside her.

"This is fabulous," she said, shaking water from her face, and spraying him with the water from her ponytail.

He laughed and splashed her. In only seconds a full-fledge water fight was under way. Finally Bethanne cried to stop. She was laughing so hard she was swallowing water.

She began to cough and Rashid was there in an instant, supporting her in the water, pounding on her back.

"I'm okay," she gasped a minute later. "I shouldn't be laughing when I'm being deluged by tidal waves."

"I haven't played like that in a long time," Rashid said as they began slowly swimming back toward the boat.

"You should. I think you work too hard."

"Ah, maybe it's the company I'm keeping. Makes it more fun."

She glowed with the compliment. From a rocky beginning, it looked as if things were changing.

"I could say the same. I've enjoyed being here."

"It won't be much longer."

She felt her heart drop. "How close are you to completing your deal?" she asked, almost fearing the answer.

"Close enough to expect to sign the papers this week."

Bethanne felt the disappointment like an anchor in her chest. She actually faltered a moment in swimming. What had she expected—that it would take years to sign the contracts?

"I hope you won't dash off the instant the ink hits the paper," Rashid said.

They reached the boat. He steadied the ladder while she climbed. Once she was on board, he swiftly followed.

"I need to return to Texas," she said slowly. She could stay a few days, maybe, yet to what end? She could go sightseeing on her own, but it wouldn't be the same as with Rashid. And he had to believe her father had taken the plane, no matter what the man on the platform had said. He'd mentioned it often enough. Had she misunderstood Hasid?

"I could stay for a little longer." Was that breathless voice hers? Those foolish dreams lingering?

"Because?" he pressed.

"Because I want to."

Rashid smiled in satisfaction, then pulled her gently into his arms to kiss her.

His warm body pressed against hers as the boat bobbed on the sea, his arms holding her so she didn't lose her balance. Her own arms soon went around his neck as she savored every inch of contact. She was in love with the most exciting man she'd ever known. And he hadn't a clue.

* * *

They dined together on the veranda. As twilight fell, Bethanne felt as if she couldn't hold so much happiness. The conversation was lively and fun. She wondered who else saw this side of the man.

"How come you aren't married?" she asked at one point, wondering why some smart woman hadn't latched on to him years ago.

The atmosphere changed in an instant. His demeanor hardened. "The woman I planned to marry ran off, remember?"

"Come on, you're too dynamic and sexy to not have your share of women interested. How did no one capture your fancy?"

He was silent for so long Bethanne wondered what she'd said to cause the change. Wasn't it all right to question his single state?

"I was engaged a long time ago," he said slowly.

Oh, oh, she hadn't seen that coming. "What happened?" No matter what, it couldn't have a happy ending. She was bubbling with so much happiness, she wanted him to share. Now her stupid comment had changed the evening. She wished she could recapture her words.

"She loved my money."

"Ouch."

"I should have seen it coming." He looked at her. "All her conversation centered on things and trips. I was the gold at the end of her rainbow."

"She might have loved you as well?" she offered.

He shook his head. "When my father bought her off, she left like a fire exploding at the rigs. I haven't heard from her since."

Bethanne didn't know what to say. Her heart hurt for the pain of betrayal he must have felt.

"How about you? You're not married," he said a moment later.

"I'm footloose and fancy free. I don't see settling down

when there is the entire world to see. Working with Starcraft, I get the chance to explore places I haven't been." Besides, I have never fallen in love before, she thought, watching him. And I don't expect to find another like you.

"You don't see yourself settling down, making a family?" he asked.

"If I meet the right guy, I guess I would," she said. "If he loved me in return." For too long she'd considered herself like her father—too interested in the wide world to settle for one spot. Now that she met Rashid, she sure didn't feel that way. She'd traveled to every continent on the globe. Made friends in various places. Yet nothing drew her like Rashid. Maybe that was the difference falling in love made.

Rashid nodded, wondering why he cared if she settled down or not. He was not interested in marriage. He'd agreed to the scheme with Haile as a business move. Her defection saved him. He would be grateful to her on two counts—keeping him single, and introducing Bethanne into his life.

She was different from women he knew. That was the novelty of being around her. Soon the novelty would fade and he'd move on. He didn't want to think like a cynic, but he had no expectations of falling in love. He wanted Bethanne, liked being with her. But surely there was more to love than that.

She was a refreshing break from the routine of his life. One he didn't want to end too soon. It didn't hurt that she was so pretty. He enjoyed watching her. Or taking her to events. She looked relaxed and pleased with life in the blue dress she wore. He would love to adorn her with jewels, but she'd carefully returned the sapphire necklace once they returned to the villa after the polo dinner. He'd offered for her to keep the necklace, but she'd refused.

He should have told Khalid that. Maybe knowing Bethanne better, he'd realize his assessment was off. She wanted nothing personal from this charade. She was almost too good to be true. But he'd seen no sign of avarice in her.

He stared out across the garden, wondering about Hasid's comments to her. The old man couldn't know more about Hank than he did. Hank had worked for his father. In the morning he'd have his assistant find out more about the wild story the man had told Bethanne.

"I need to fly to Morocco on Friday to sign the contract."

She sipped her coffee before nodding. "Then I'll ask for a few more days of vacation so I can stay a bit longer," she replied.

He was pleased she agreed to stay. Maybe he'd take time from work and spend it all with Bethanne before she left for good.

The thought of her departure weighed heavily. Yet he knew better than she that there was no long-term future for them together. His family would never accept the daughter of a thief—moreover the one whose actions contributed to his father's death. She didn't speak his language. He didn't want a wife. And he would not dishonor her by having an affair. Time together, memories made, then goodbye.

His gaze shifted to her as she sipped the hot tea. She loved flying. And he couldn't see asking her to stop. It was a novelty to have her fly his plane. Maybe he could hire her to fly for him—his private pilot. That way she'd always be around. And when he needed to travel, Bethanne would travel with him.

"After Morocco we could fly on to Paris, if you like," he said. He knew women around the world loved Paris.

"That would be nice."

"You don't sound as excited as I thought you'd be."

"I haven't seen Paris with you. That would make it special," she said slowly. "I enjoyed our excursion into the western part of your country. Maybe another trip there?"

"Quraim Wadi Samil? It's hardly a hot spot. Not a place we would have gone had Alexes not needed immediate medical attention."

She faced him. "It hardly matters where we go, if we're together, don't you think?"

He wanted her as he had wanted no other woman. Not even Marguerite. But caution held him back.

"It doesn't matter, as long as we're together," he said, already regretting the day they would say goodbye.

CHAPTER SEVEN

RASHID answered the phone the next morning when his assistant told him it was Khalid.

"So the deal is done. You've both signed?" his brother asked without amenities.

"I'm flying to Morocco on Friday to sign with Benqura. Then it is done. And a better deal than expected, thanks to his daughter's flight. He needs to save face and I've assured him I will handle things on this end."

"And how to explain to the minister that your special friend Bethanne left?"

"I don't have to explain anytime soon."

"Because?"

"I've asked her to stay. I may offer her a pilot's job. Alexes will not be able to fly again. Another stroke could happen at any time."

"There are other pilots who work for us."

"I choose who will fly my planes."

"Fly your planes and warm your bed."

"Hardly that. Bethanne and I are not involved to that extent," Rashid said coldly. Not for lack of desire on his part. Bethanne was special, and he would treat her so. For as long as it suited him. And her.

"She wants something. Mark my words."

"And what does it take to prove you wrong—her friendship and loyalty for fifty years?" He knew what Bethanne wanted. It was impossible to give it to her. Beyond that, she cared for nothing he had to offer.

"That's a start."

Rashid laughed. "Give it up, Khalid. She is not like the others."

A groan sounded. "You are too far gone. All women are alike."

"Cynic. Is that why you called—just to warn me again about her?"

"No, I'm going to open Grandmother's other house. I can't decide whether to live there or sell it. So I thought if I stayed there a few weeks, I'd know what I want to do. It's strange to go there without her."

"She wanted you to have it, Khalid. She loved that house because it was her father's that he gave to her when she married."

"My flat suits me. I'm not in it long enough to feel closed in."

"Give it a fair chance. You don't have to rush into selling."

When Rashid hung up, he thought about his brother. Life had treated them so differently. Both had the same advantages until the fire had destroyed part of his brother. It wasn't only the scar. There were wounds that went deeper. Were the al Harum men doomed to stay single? Not leave heirs on the earth?

How would he fare if he took that step? What if he considered marriage with someone like Bethanne? Their children would be beautiful. She'd be full of surprises for a long time. Would they agree on how to focus their lives, or always want something different?

Not liking the way his thoughts were going, he picked up a report and refused to think about her for the rest of the morning.

Easier said than done, he admitted a few moments later. He

didn't believe Khalid. His brother had not been around Bethanne long enough to know her. Yet that shadow of doubt wouldn't fade. Marguerite had seemed devoted, until offered a sum of money. Would Bethanne prove as shallow?

Restless, he checked his calendar. There was nothing pressing. Telling his assistant he was going to take the rest of the day off, he headed for the villa. He wanted to see her, spend time with her. Assuage the doubt and prove once and for all she was different.

Prove to Khalid that Bethanne was unique.

When Rashid reached the villa it was to find Bethanne had gone out.

"Where?" he asked the maid. Maybe he should have kept Fatima to watch her.

But Bethanne wasn't a prisoner. She was free to go where she wished.

"She received a note and then asked if Teaz could drive her to the city," Minnah said. "I don't know when she will return."

Rashid nodded and went into the study. Using his mobile phone, he called the driver.

"Where are you?" he asked when Teaz answered.

Hearing they were in old town, Rashid arranged for Teaz to stay there until he arrived. He'd enjoy showing Bethanne some of the history of the capital city. She'd enjoyed Quraim Wadi Samil; he was sure she'd enjoy the architecture of the Romula district.

When Rashid pulled in behind his limo, driving his own small sports car, Teaz climbed out and came to open his door.

"Where is she?"

"I stop here. She walks to the square," Teaz said.

"You're dismissed. I'll bring her back to the villa."

The chauffeur bowed and returned to the limo.

Rashid walked toward the square. It brought back memories. Hank Pendarvis had lived in this area of town. He remembered that. His father had thought so highly of him. His assistant had not yet contacted Hasid. What if there was some truth to the old man's story? Could Hank have crashed? It still did not explain why he stole the plane.

When Rashid reached the square he paused for a moment, searching. Her blond head was quickly found. She sat at a table with an older man. From the way they were talking, Rashid knew they weren't strangers. Who was he?

The spurt of jealousy that hit him surprised him. He didn't want to admit he had stronger feelings for her. But seeing her laugh at something her companion said jarred him. He wanted her laughter and her smiles. He wanted her.

Walking around the square, his gaze never left them. They were so caught up in their conversation, neither looked up until he stopped at the table.

Bethanne's eyes widened when she saw him. For a moment anger burned. He realized he was used to seeing a spurt of happiness when he came near. Now she looked startled—guilty? He kept his anger under control. The first rule—find out the facts before acting. Nothing so far condemned her.

"Hi, Rashid. I didn't expect to see you here," she said with a quick glance at her companion.

"Probably not." He looked at the other man.

"This is Walt Hampstead. He teaches English at the university," Bethanne said quickly. "Walt, this is my host, Sheikh Rashid al Harum."

Host? They were pretending more than that. To everyone.

The man rose and extended his hand. "Sheikh al Harum. It's a pleasure to meet you."

Rashid shook hands and then looked at Bethanne. "The man who knew your father?"

She nodded. "Do join us. We were talking about mutual friends." She gathered the photographs displayed in front of her and stacked them, handing them back to Walt. He put them in an envelope before Rashid could see them.

"I was showing her pictures of my family. It's good to talk to Hank's daughter. I don't see many Americans in Quishari, you know," he said easily, tapping the envelope against his leg.

"You have lived here long?" Rashid asked.

"Almost twenty years. Married a local girl. We have two children—teenagers now." He glanced at Bethanne. "I hope to see you again soon. Thanks for the update."

Bethanne smiled and nodded, her glance flicking to Rashid.

"I did not mean to run you off," he said.

"I need to be going. Classes soon." Walt nodded once and quickly walked across the square and down one of the side roads.

Rashid pulled out a chair and sat. The waiter hurried over and asked if he wanted anything.

"I'll have a coffee," he said, leaning back. His curiosity rose. "What was really going on?"

Bethanne looked at him, her eyes wide. "He knew my father. He doesn't believe my father stole a plane, either."

When his coffee was delivered, he took a sip of the hot beverage. Bethanne fidgeted with her own coffee cup, now nearly empty.

"What are you doing here?" she asked at last.

"I thought I'd take you up on your offer to take some time off. I expected to find you at the villa."

"I still want to see as much as Alkaahdar as I can. Wander around town. This is a nice café."

"We can wander around old town if you like. I sent Teaz away. I drove."

"Lovely. The architecture is similar to that in Quraim Wadi Samil, don't you think?"

"It's from the same age."

They finished their coffee and started out. The stalls selling food were crowded. The others had vendors calling out, enticing people with special sales. Bethanne smiled and walked at his side. When they reached a cross street, he waited to see what she'd do. She appeared to be studying the architecture as if she were genuinely interested. Rashid watched her. He was still bothered by the encounter with the other man. She was tenacious in searching for Hank. She was not one to give up quickly. He wondered how she'd found the man who had known Hank.

A woman came from an apartment building. Rashid stepped aside to allow her to pass on the narrow sidewalk. When she saw Rashid's gesture, she smiled as she walked past—stopping suddenly when she saw Bethanne.

"Were you coming to see me?" she said in Arabic.

"No. Should I be?" Rashid asked, wondering who she was.

"The woman was here in the street a few days ago searching for the man who had the flat before me. She was told I knew nothing about him. I thought maybe you were coming to seek more information. I have nothing else to add."

Bethanne watched, her eyes darting from Rashid to the woman back to him.

He looked at her.

"You were looking for more information about your father?" he asked in English.

Bethanne nodded. "I was hoping he'd left something behind that might tell me where he'd gone and why. She wasn't home last time I was here. But Walt said he came by when he hadn't seen my dad for a while and was told the apartment had been cleared before being rented again. The man on the oil rig told me he crashed. Walt said he spoke of a secret assignment, a special flight. There had to be more to it than he appropriated a plane and I want to know what. I want to know the truth. I want you to admit the truth."

He stared at her. "I would tell you if I knew more. Do you think I like knowing your father was a thief? Especially after years of service with my family? What else might he have stolen? What other harm might he have done?"

"None. He was not like that. He loved working here. We often spoke about his finding his ideal job. He planned to show me the country, introduce me to his friends. He went on some secret mission for your father. If you don't know what it is, come with me to find out what it was."

"Come with you where?"

"Quraim Wadi Samil. Isn't that where the answers lie?"

"There are no answers."

"Only questions? Like why people think he is a thief? I need to find out what happened to him."

"Everyone wants something—Khalid was right. I thought we had something developing between us. But you only see me as a way to prove the unprovable."

"We might have something growing between us. Just because the reasons I agreed to stay haven't changed doesn't mean my feelings aren't genuine or aren't involved. I...love you, Rashid."

"No!"

"If I do?"

"Impossible." He glared at her. "Please give me some credit. Women say words like that hoping to bend men to their will."

"We're talking two different things here, Rashid. First I want to prove to you my dad is not what you think. And second, why wouldn't I fall for someone like you? You're—"

"Enough! We have an agreement, nothing beyond the charade until the negotiations are complete and the contract signed. What do you hope…that I'll fall for you? Maybe see you as my wife? I would not dishonor my family by marrying a woman whose father was a thief. Who caused the death of my father."

Rashid resumed walking, at a quicker pace. He clamped down on his emotions. Khalid had been right; he should have sent her back the first day. How dare she say she loved him? He knew better—he was a means to an end. Find out about her father. Hadn't they tried that three years ago? The sooner he got her to the villa, the sooner he could be rid of her.

Except for the flight to Morocco, he thought. Should he consider using another pilot?

"Wait." She hurried to catch up. "Rashid, this doesn't change anything."

"It changes everything. Here's my car. Get in."

Ignoring his manners, he strode to the driver's side and got in just as she jumped in the passenger's side.

Starting the engine, he pulled away from the curb at a pace faster than safe. For a moment anger ruled. Then he deliberately slowed down. He would not take his anger out on others.

How dare she suggest she was in love with him? They had not known each other long enough for emotions to grow. It was a ploy, just as Khalid suggested. He was furious for letting his own emotions grow concerning her. He'd been so confident he could enjoy her company and then say farewell. She turned out to be like all others.

"What did Hampstead tell you?" he bit out.

"That the last time he saw Hank, my dad spoke about a secret mission. Walt thought he was pumped up about it, like a thriller or something. He wouldn't tell Walt any more than that. But Walt thought it more a lark than a dangerous mission. He was obviously wrong since it seems likely my dad ended up dead. The man at the derrick said Hank's buried in Quraim Wadi Samil. It would be worth checking out. Did you question him?"

"My assistant is handling that." And it sounded like Rashid needed to make sure it was done immediately. "The reason he was pumped up was probably considering stealing a multimillion-dollar jet plane."

Bethanne refused to respond.

Rashid stopped in front of the villa a short time later. She scurried out of the car before he could come around to her door. Running up the shallow steps, she turned and looked at him. "I shall leave the villa, of course. I understand you wouldn't want me here. I'll call a taxi to take me to a hotel."

"Stay here until we leave."

"We?" she asked.

"I still need to fly to Morocco tomorrow."

"And Quraim Wadi Samil?"

"Once we return, you'll have to find your own way there."

She glared at him. "Don't worry, I shall!" She turned to enter the villa.

Rashid stood standing beside his car. The door closed. She was gone.

For endless minutes he stood staring at the door, feeling numb. One moment she says she loves him. The next she's talking about leaving. The images of them together over the last few days danced in his mind. He could almost hear her laughter, see the sparkle in her eyes. For the first time since Marguerite he'd let himself consider— No, he was not going there.

He clenched a fist and hit the top of the car. He'd been thinking of ways to keep her in Quishari, and she'd been playing him. At least she had no idea he'd been halfway falling in love with her.

It was a small solace.

* * *

Bethanne reached her bedroom and shut the door. Sinking on her bed, she blinked her eyes. She would not cry. But the heartbreak she'd feared was closing in. Rashid had been so annoyed. Why? It wasn't as if he hadn't known from the beginning she was searching for her father. She should not have confessed her feelings. He hadn't wanted any emotional entanglements. He was probably laughing all the way back to the city about her claim. Her throat ached with keeping back the tears.

His reaction was unexpected. How could he feel so strongly about his own family and not recognize the same bond she had for hers?

She loved him. She hadn't meant to tell him, not without some indication he might be feeling something for her. But she had blurted it out. And he threw it back in her face. She did not want to go to Morocco or ever be around him again. How embarrassing that would be. Oh, if only she could go back in time a few hours and change everything.

She jumped up and began to pace the spacious area between her bed and the French doors. Rubbing her chest, she tried to erase the ache that was growing in her heart. She had warned herself repeatedly. But no matter—she'd fallen in love with a man who had never given any hint he returned her feelings. If he thought she was as dishonorable as he thought her father, he never would. Despite the kisses they'd shared.

Her father had been an honorable man. She resented the fact people thought he'd stolen a valuable plane and disappeared. She wanted the world to know the truth.

And she wanted Rashid to fall in love with her—daughter of a thief or not.

She might as well wish for the moon.

* * *

Minnah came into the room some time later with a message the sheikh had moved up the departure for Morocco to the next morning. They would depart at six.

Bethanne accepted her visit to Quishari was over. She'd fly the sheikh to sign his important contract, return to Quishari and be on the next commercial flight to the United States.

Packing, she took only those clothes she'd brought. She fingered the beautiful dresses that hung in the closet. She had felt like a princess wearing them. Who would wear them next? Would he donate to a charity or dump in the trash?

Taking advantage of her last afternoon, she went to the beach. Walking eased some of her distress. She was still trying to figure out a way to get to Quraim Wadi Samil when she looked up and saw Rashid.

Her traitorous heart gave a leap of happiness when she saw him, even though his face was grave. When would she get over this feeling of delight in his presence?

"Is something wrong?" she asked when he got closer.

"My mother is having a small dinner party tonight and insists we attend." The muscles in his cheeks clenched with anger.

Bethanne hadn't expected that. She searched his face for a clue he also wanted to attend. He glared at her. No hope there.

"Surely you can tell her about the charade. She wouldn't expect us to attend after finding out about that," she said.

"The minister and his wife will be there. The contracts are not yet signed. I will do nothing to jeopardize this deal. Not having come this far."

"Of course. The deal. No matter what."

"Nothing's changed. Except my perception of your cooperation. If you do anything tonight to enlighten anyone, you'll be sorry."

"Gee, what will you do? Send me back to the U.S.? Banish me from the country I'm leaving anyway?" An imp of mischief goaded her. She wanted him to want her. As she'd thought his kisses had indicated. So be it that he had not fallen in love with her as she had with him. She would not go off like some quiet, docile child. He was a wonderful man. Her love was not returned, but it didn't make it wrong, just sad that the one man she'd found she'd want to build a life with had no similar feelings for her.

"Don't push me, Bethanne."

"You have something I want. I have something you want. Let's make a deal."

"You have nothing I want."

"My silence. My continued acting like a love-struck woman clinging to your every word—especially if the minister is present."

He looked out to the sea.

"And in return, I want a plane ride to Quraim Wadi Samil. We swap."

He was silent for so long she knew he was going to refuse. She had no other leverage. She would have to find the grave herself—if in fact it was there.

"Deal."

His answer surprised her. Before he could change his mind, she held out her hand, but when he turned back, it was to grab her shoulders and draw her close enough to kiss. It wasn't a sweet kiss, but one full of anger. His mouth pressed hard against hers. His fingers gripped tightly. She scarcely caught a breath before he released her a second later. No matter, her heart pounded.

"Consider the deal sealed," he said and turned to head toward the villa.

"I'll pick you up at six-thirty," he called over his shoulder.

She brushed her fingertips across her lips. Tears filled her eyes. She wanted kisses, but not punishing ones. Could she ever forget the passionate ones they'd shared? She was afraid she never would. All men in the future would come short when compared with Sheikh Rashid al Harum.

"I hope your deal brings you joy. Nothing else seems to," she said to the empty beach.

Bethanne took extra care getting ready for her farewell performance, as she termed it. She had Minnah style her hair and selected the prettiest of the gowns hanging in the closet. It was a deep burgundy, long and sleek. Her makeup was donned for impact, making her eyes look larger and mysterious. She matched the gown color with lipstick and studied the dramatic effect in the mirror.

"Eat your heart out, Rashid," she whispered.

She went downstairs to await her escort. When he arrived, she met him at the door. "I'm ready," she said, walking past, head held high. She planned to deliver exactly what he wanted: a woman infatuated with him—when in public.

Teaz stood at the back door of the limo. Once she was seated, Rashid joined her on the bench seat. The ride was conducted in total silence.

Once at his mother's, Rashid morphed into a charming host. He greeted the other guests, introducing Bethanne to those she hadn't met before. She was gracious and friendly. She was never going to give him a single reason to think of her as less than professional in all her dealings. Her greeting to Madame al Harum was warm, as she felt suitable to a prospective mother-in-law. The older woman did not thaw at her overtures. Bethanne merely smiled. She would never please her. And tonight she had no reason to even pretend.

She greeted the minister again. Tonight she met his wife. The woman did not speak English, so Rashid translated. When they moved on, she breathed a sigh of relief. So far so good.

Conversation was a mixture of Arabic, French and English. She had a nice chat with a young diplomatic couple, on their way to a post in Egypt. The minister of finance was no more friendly than he'd been at the polo event. She wondered if he were perpetually grumpy. She wished Walt had been invited. It would have been nice to have one friendly face in the group.

Dinner was traditional Arabic fare—from an avocado appetizer to the delicious lamb to the sweets at the conclusion. Bethanne enjoyed every bite. She especially liked the sugared walnuts that Rashid insisted be brought for her enjoyment. She smiled her appreciation, wishing he'd meant the gesture for more than show to the people present. To the rest of them, she was sure they looked like a couple who enjoyed each other's company. Maybe were in love.

Only the two of them knew the lie behind the facade. It was bittersweet to have him so attentive, when she knew by the look in his eyes how false it was. She met him gaze for gaze, tilting her chin up to convey she had no qualms of standing up for herself. Or defending her stance. He'd asked her to stay to foil the attempts of the opposition to bring an end to negotiations. She'd done just that. He had not asked for more. It was her own foolish heart that betrayed her—not him.

The company moved to the salon and terrace after dinner. Soft music played in the background. The view from the terrace was beautiful; the entire city of Alkaahdar spread out before them, lighted in the darkness. In the distance, the Persian Gulf, where a lone ship gleamed with lights as it slid silently along on the horizon.

She would miss this place, she realized. In the short time she'd been here, she'd fallen in love with Quishari and one very special person. Her father had loved this country and she felt the same.

She realized she was alone on the terrace when Madame al Harum came to stand beside her.

"You are leaving," she said.

"Yes. We fly to Morocco tomorrow. When we return to Quishari, I will fly home."

"It is good."

"I'm sure you think so. What if Rashid loved me? Do you think a broken heart is good?" she asked.

"He would never be so foolish to marry someone so unsuitable. It's obvious you have fallen for him, but my son knows his duty. He will marry to suit his family. It is the duty of children to honor their parents."

"It is a bit old-fashioned," Bethanne said gently. "We honor our parents, but don't marry to please them."

"We are a traditional country. We have the modern conveniences necessary to enjoy life, but our values are time-honored. My son does not need you."

Bethanne nodded, the thought piercing. "You are right. I'm leaving and you will be happier for it, right?"

The older woman stared at her for a long time, then looked out toward the sea. "I will be content. It is what I want."

Bethanne longed to ask her if she missed her husband. Hadn't they been love? If not when first married, had love come? No matter what the custom, it had to be awkward to marry if not in love. Yet the union had produced two dynamic men. Had she longed for a daughter? For grandchildren?

Bethanne had once thought she'd never marry. She'd been fooling herself. If Rashid asked her, she'd say yes in a heartbeat. Her declarations of independence had been made before falling in love. The world changed when that happened.

Even if the ending wasn't happy.

"Mother, one of your guests is leaving," Rashid said from the doorway.

She turned and smiled politely at Bethanne. "If I do not see you again, have a pleasant flight home."

"Goodbye, Madame," Bethanne replied.

Rashid stepped onto the terrace. "Are you ready to leave?"

"Anytime. Your mother can't wait for me to be gone. I'm glad this pretense will end soon. I'm thinking it never should have begun."

But then she would not have spent but ten minutes with Rashid while he signed the papers for the new jet. She'd have missed these days which, despite the circumstances, would remain some of the happiest of her life.

"The past can never be changed," Rashid said.

The future could. But she refused to cling to false hope.

Bethanne arrived at the airport before the sheikh the next morning. She checked with the ground crew and had visually inspected the aircraft before he arrived. Her flight bag was already stowed. Teaz loaded a small suitcase for Rashid and then drove away. Rashid brought a briefcase and was soon seated on the sofa, papers already pulled out to review.

"The weather outlook is good the entire way," she said. "We'll have a refueling stop in Cairo."

He nodded and Bethanne went to the cockpit to begin her preflight checklist. They were soon airborne. She watched as the land moved beneath her. She was not familiar enough with it to recognize landmarks. Somewhere below them soon would be the oasis in the desert where her father lay. She was not going home without stopping there. Maybe she'd ask Khalid to find out from Hasid where exactly her father was buried. If he knew she were leaving, he might be amenable to helping her.

As the hours slipped by, the topography changed. The hills and valleys gave way to mountains. Crossing over a while later, the blue of the Mediterranean Sea could be seen in the distance.

It was late afternoon Morocco time when she approached the runway of Menara Airport, serving Marrakech.

It had been a long day. They'd refueled in Cairo where Bethanne had stretched her legs for a while. The flight had not brought the usual delight. She dwelled on the vanished hope the two of them might come to mean more to each other. It was also a bit lonely without someone to share the cockpit with. She would love to talk about the beauty of the earth below or the freedom flying usually gave her.

Rashid remained in the cabin. He'd declined to get off in Cairo. She had hoped for some kind of truce, but he obviously wasn't of the same mind.

She followed the directions from the tower and pulled the jet to a stop near a private hangar on the edge of the vast airport. Cutting the engines, she leaned back in her seat and closed her eyes for a moment. She was tired—not just from the long flight but from the emotional toll of the last two days.

Garnering what energy she could, she finished her check-list, signed it and left the clipboard on the copilot's seat. Going to the door, she opened it and stood aside, waiting for Rashid to leave.

He carried his briefcase and headed down the stairs, where there was already a chauffeured limousine for his use. She wondered how all the details of such precision were conveyed. She knew his staff was efficient, but this seemed almost miraculous.

When the uniformed chauffeur saw him into the back of the car, he came to the plane to retrieve the sheikh's suitcase. He nodded briefly to Bethanne, but didn't say a word. She stood back and watched as the limo pulled away.

If she had not told him about her feelings, or if he had believed her, she would be going with him, meeting the man whose daughter caused the charade. There was no need to keep up the pretense here where no one from his country could see. Once the contracts were signed, it would no longer matter.

She sighed and turned to check the cabin. It was as neat and tidy as if she'd flown it empty.

A maintenance worker came aboard, saying something in Arabic.

She replied in English. He shook his head, so she tried French. That he understood and explained he'd come to clean the interior. She told him to go ahead, but she'd wait until he was done. In fact, Bethanne wasn't sure what she would do. Stay with the plane was her inclination. She had no hotel reservations, hadn't a clue how to get a cab to this isolated area of the airport, didn't know how to find a place to stay since she couldn't speak the language. She could sleep on the sofa. Food and beverages stocked the refrigerator.

"And as the ranking crew member present on the plane, what I say goes," she murmured. When the maintenance worker left, she activated the door, retracting the steps and closing it. Cocooned in the aircraft, she hunted up a magazine and went to flop down on the sofa. In less than ten minutes she was asleep.

Rashid registered at the hotel, paid for a second room for Bethanne's use and sent the limo driver back to get her. It was petty to leave her like that, but he was still angry—more with himself than her. She had things to do when a plane landed, so the timing would probably be perfect.

He checked out his suite, found it satisfactory. Truth be told it could have been a hovel and he wouldn't have cared. Leaving it behind, he went to find a decent restaurant for an early dinner and to finalize his strategy for tomorrow's meeting.

When Rashid returned to the hotel, it was after ten. He'd had a leisurely meal, then gone to a small coffeehouse to work on the final details of the deal he and al Benqura would sign the next day. Walking back to the hotel, he enjoyed the atmosphere of Marrakech. He'd visited as a younger man on holiday one summer. The walk brought back memories.

He crossed the lobby heading for the elevators when the desk clerk called him.

"Yes?"

"Message for you, sir," he said.

Rashid went to the counter and took the folded paper. Scanning it as he started for the elevators, he stopped.

"When was this delivered?" he asked, turning back.

"A bit before six. It's written on the back."

He murmured an expletive. The note explained Bethanne had not been at the plane when the chauffeur arrived. The door was closed and no one had seen her since the arrival. Crossing to the house phone discreetly located in a quiet corner, Rashid dialed the number on the note. The car service was closed for the day. Crushing the paper in his hand, he went outside and asked the doorman to hail a cab.

CHAPTER EIGHT

WHERE could she have gone? She didn't know anyone in Marrakech. Not that he knew of. Of course she had a life apart from the few days she'd spent in Quishari. Maybe she had a host of friends here.

But she'd said nothing about that when they'd first discussed the flight.

The cabdriver was reluctant to go to the section of the airport Rashid directed. An extra handful of coins changed his mind. The hangar had a light on inside, scarcely enough illumination to see the door. The jet was parked nearby, where it had been that afternoon. It was dark inside. The door was closed. How had she managed that from the ground?

A lone guard came out of a small office, alert with hand poised on a gun worn at his side.

"Sir? This is private property," he said when Rashid got out of the cab.

"This is my jet. I am Sheikh Rashid al Harum. I arrived this afternoon."

"What are you doing here now, sir?" the man asked, still suspicious.

"I'm looking for my pilot."

The man looked surprised. He glanced around. "There's no

one here but me. The maintenance workers come back in the morning. I haven't seen a pilot."

"I need to know where she went," Rashid said.

"She? The pilot is a woman?" the man exclaimed in surprise.

"Yes. Who do you call if there is a problem?"

"What problem?"

"Like a missing pilot," Rashid said, leaning closer. The guard took a step back.

"I will call."

Rashid followed him to the small office. In a few moments he was talking to one of the men who worked the special planes. He had not serviced the private jet but knew who had. He'd call him to find out if he knew where the pilot was.

Rashid had his answer in less than five minutes.

"Open the door," he instructed the guard, walking back to the jet.

"I do not know how," he said, following along.

Rashid cupped his hands and yelled for Bethanne. He heard only the background noise from the busy part of the airport. This was futile. The jet was insulated; she couldn't hear a call.

"Bring a ramp."

"A ramp?"

Rashid was getting frustrated with the echoing by the guard.

"Yes, I want to open that door from the outside. I'm not tall enough standing on the tarmac." He was losing his patience trying to determine if Bethanne was indeed on board the jet.

Beckoning the cabdriver, the three men pushed a ramp in place, ramming it into the side of the jet as they tried to line it up next to the door, so as not to interfere with the steps coming down if he was successful in opening it.

He started up the steps but before he reached the top platform, the door to the jet opened, the stairs slowly unfolding. Bethanne stood in the opening.

"Rashid, what in the world are you doing?"

"Trying to find you. I sent the limo back for you but the fool driver didn't see you so left. What are you doing here?"

"I was asleep." She frowned as she looked at the ramp and the two men at the foot of it. "Your crashing into the side of the plane woke me. I hope you haven't scratched or dented it."

"Doesn't matter. It's my plane. Come on. The taxi is waiting."

"Come on where?" she asked warily.

"I booked you a room at the hotel I'm using."

He walked back down the ramp and thanked the two men who had helped him, giving each of them a folded bill. From the look of surprise on one and gratification on the other, he was satisfied they'd been amply rewarded for their help.

Bethanne still stood in the doorway, indecision evident in her expression.

Rashid hoped he wouldn't have to use stronger measures to get her to the cab. But he was not leaving her to spend the night in the jet. Unless he stayed with her.

She ducked back inside and a moment later tossed her bag over the railing of the movable ramp. Stepping over herself, she reached back and initiated the mechanism that closed the jet's door. When the plane was secure, she picked up her bag and walked slowly down the stairs.

"I'm guarding the plane," the guard said when she reached the tarmac. "No one will get on it tonight."

She looked at Rashid with a question in her eyes.

He translated for her and she smiled at the guard, saying in her newly learned Arabic, "Thank you."

Rashid took her bag and handed it to the cabdriver. Taking her hand, he helped her into the back of the cab and climbed in next to her.

"You can't have thought I would leave you to fend for yourself in a country where you don't speak the language," he said gruffly as the driver started the engine and they pulled away from the maintenance hangar.

"You're angry at me. Why not?"

He looked at her. "Bethanne, anger or not, I wouldn't do such a thing."

She nodded. He was not reassured.

"It is quite a few hours after you left," she said.

"I went to dinner. When I returned to the hotel, I learned you had not checked in. It's taken me all this time to find you."

"I appreciate it, but I was fine in the jet. It has all the conveniences of home."

When they arrived at the hotel, Rashid accompanied her to her room. Once he'd checked it out, he went to the door. "I'm in suite 1735. Call me if you need anything."

"Thank you for the room. What time do we leave tomorrow?"

"My meeting with al Benqura is at ten. I expect to be finished before noon. Perhaps you'd care to explore Marrakech before we leave."

"I'll do that in the morning, and be at the plane by noon," she said, standing near the window.

As if putting as much distance between them, he thought. "I meant, explore together. I was here about twelve years ago. I wouldn't mind seeing some of the souks and the Medina again."

"With me?" Her surprise was exaggerated.

He debated arguing with her, but decided against it.

"I'll meet you here at the hotel at noon." He left before she could protest.

Bethanne watched the door shut behind Rashid. She didn't know what to make of his coming to find her. She would have been okay all night on the jet. She'd slept in worse places. And she did not want to feel special because of the determination he'd displayed in locating her. But it touched her heart. She blinked back tears. She'd so love to have him always look after her. To know she was special to him in a unique way.

Taking a quick shower, she went to bed. It was more comfortable than the sofa for a night's sleep, she thought as she drifted off.

The next morning she ordered room service. She sat at the table next to the window, wishing she had a balcony and a sea breeze. Which would be hard to do in Marrakech, which was located far from the sea. She gazed out her window at the newer buildings, anticipating the afternoon tour of the old section, the Medina.

Bethanne went down to the lobby shortly before noon. She sat on one of the plush sofas and people-watched. It was a favorite activity. She wished she spoke the languages she heard. There were a variety, from Arabic to French to German and Spanish.

She saw Rashid the instant he entered through the revolving doors. He strode directly toward the elevators and she wondered if she should call him or let him deposit the briefcase and then let him know she was here. As if she had spoken, however, he looked directly at her. He walked over.

"So did you get it signed?" she asked as she stood.

"I did." The quiet satisfaction showed her more than anything that he was pleased with the deal.

"Good."

His eyes stared into hers. For a second, Bethanne felt the surroundings fade. There was only Rashid in her sight. Then sanity returned and she blinked, looking away.

"I know you want to ditch the briefcase. I'll wait here."

"I can send it up to the room," he said. "Ready to go?"

"Yes."

He gave the briefcase to the bell captain with instructions to deliver to his suite. Then he offered his arm to Bethanne.

The gesture surprised her. It was almost as if he were continuing their pretense.

She glanced down at the uniform she wore and slowly shook her head.

He reached for her hand and drew it through the crook of her arm.

"I'm hardly dressed like a woman going out with someone," she said.

"You look fine. Al Benqura has invited us to dine with him tonight. I said I had to make sure you wanted to do so."

"Do you want to?" she asked, surprised by the invitation.

"It would be a nice gesture to wind up the negotiations and the signed deal. But if you say no, I'll decline."

"I have nothing to wear."

He laughed sardonically. "Classic woman's response."

Bethanne looked at him. "Am I missing something? You were so angry the other day I thought you'd have a fit. Now you're like Mr. Nice Guy. What's going on?"

He didn't reply until they were in the back of the limousine she'd seen yesterday.

"I'm afraid I let the pretense go further than it should," he said cryptically. "You did your part. There was never anything more I could have expected. So today is about exploring Marrakech and seeing the sights. Tomorrow we'll return to Quishari and you'll be free to return home."

"So today we celebrate success," she said, disappointed at his explanation. She wanted more. She wanted him to say he couldn't let her go. That he'd fallen in love with her as she had with him. That he believed in her no matter what.

Only, today was merely a reward for a pretense well done. Some of the sparkle and anticipation dimmed.

Still—if today was all she had, she'd take it. Make more memories to treasure down through the years. Maybe she could pretend for just a few hours that they still enjoyed the camaraderie they had before. They were both away from home, no one to see or hear. She would be herself and hope he'd at least come to realize she had not lied or been dishonorable in any way. She wanted him to remember her well even if he couldn't love her.

First Rashid had the driver crisscross through town, pointing out places of interest, telling her a little about when he'd visited before.

They stopped at a hotel with a renowned restaurant on top where they had lunch. Then it was to the old fortified section of town, the Medina. Because of the crowd, Rashid took her hand firmly in his as they walked along the narrow streets. The souk was also crowded with vendors and tourists and shoppers. The wares were far more varied than the ones at the square in Rumola near where her father had lived. Bethanne stopped to look at brass and some of the beautiful rugs. She ran her hands over the bolts of silks and linens for sale. Whenever Rashid suggested she buy something, she merely smiled and shook her head.

Late in the afternoon they ended up in the large square of Djemaa el Fna.

"This is said to be the largest open-air market in north Africa," Rashid said.

There were stalls selling orange juice and water. Food and flowers. Acrobats performed on colorful mats. A snake charmer caught her eye and she watched for several moments as he mesmerized crowds with his ability. The atmosphere was festive.

"Is it a holiday or something?" she asked.

"No, it's always like this. It was when I was here last."

They walked around, ending up in a sidewalk café on a side street that was just a bit less noisy and hectic. Ordering cold drinks, they sat in companionable silence for several moments.

"Thank you," she said.

"For?"

"For today."

For a moment she feared she'd shattered the mood, but he quickly looked away and she wasn't sure she'd seen a flash of anger in his eyes.

"Today has been enjoyable. Tonight we dine with al Benqura."

"I still don't have a dress," she said, sipping her iced drink.

"One will be at the hotel when we return."

She gazed across the amazing square. "It must be nice."

"What?"

"To wave your hand and have things taken care of. You live a charmed life, Rashid."

He stared at her for a long moment. "No, Bethanne. You see only the surface. I live a life like others, maybe not the majority of the world, but others of my station. We have heartaches and disappointments like any other men."

"Like what?"

He hesitated, took a sip of his own drink and then put the glass down.

"I thought I was in love when I was in my early twenties. Marguerite was beautiful, sophisticated and fun to be with. We shared so much—or so I thought. I told you before that my father bought her off. That taught me forever that love is an illusion. I cannot depend on it."

"Wrong. You may have loved her. She didn't love you. But that doesn't negate love. You are the better person for having loved her. I know it must have hurt when she left. But would you trade those feelings for money? Would you pretend to care for someone and be only out for money?"

"People can pretend and be out for other things."

She nodded. "Or maybe they don't pretend. Maybe things

become real. Love is not rationed. It is available for all. And I don't believe there is only one love in all the world for each of us. I think we have the possibility of falling in love with the wrong person as well as the right person."

"So how does one know who is the right person?"

She shrugged. "I can't say. It's just there." She knew Rashid was her right person. She wished she was his.

"Never in love?" he asked.

"Only once. For me it was the right person," she replied slowly.

"What happened?"

"He doesn't love me back," she said, her gaze on her glass. "But I wouldn't trade a moment of being together. I can't make someone love me. I will always have memories of happy hours spent together. And just maybe, because I loved once, I will love again and be happy."

After a long silent moment, he said slowly, "I wish that for you."

She nodded, blinking lest the tears that threatened spilled over. She'd told the truth. She loved him and would have happily spent the rest of her life with Rashid. But if that was not meant to be, she hoped some day in the future she'd find another man to love.

Though she wondered if it would ever be the same.

True to his word, a lovely dress awaited her when they returned to the hotel. It was white, shot through with gold. A golden necklace and golden slippers were part of the package. She felt like a princess in the lovely clothes. No matter what, she'd go with her head held high. She really wanted to meet the father of the woman Rashid might have married. Would there be any mention of that tonight?

The dinner surprised her. She expected only another couple

or two, but there were thirty couples. The dinner was a lavish affair with servants scurrying to carry in the dishes, remove dirty plates and make sure everything went smoothly.

Because she could not speak Arabic, Bethanne sat next to Rashid. But she noticed other couples were separated to mingle with the other guests.

"I'm content to eat and watch. You don't have to translate everything for me," she said softly after about ten minutes of his commenting on what others said.

"You'll be left out."

She looked at him in exasperation. "Rashid, I would never fit in here. I'm delighted to taste some more dishes and watch the other women in their finery. But I don't expect to become friends with anyone. Enjoy yourself. Truly, I'm happy enough."

Sheikh al Benqura was not like Bethanne's image. To her he looked like a father who had been disappointed in his only child. His gray hair was worn a bit long. His wife looked sad—especially every time her gaze landed on Rashid. Bethanne knew they had both wanted the marriage. Still, they were doing their best now to smooth things over. Rashid had told them he and Bethanne had a special friendship. It was true to a certain degree, but not to the level they suspected. Clever use of words, she thought.

After dinner, they stayed for only a short time, claiming an early departure time in the morning as a reason to be the first to leave.

"That went better than I expected," Rashid said as they settled in the limo for the ride back to the hotel.

"Did it?"

"Yes. You played the part perfectly. Madame al Benqura wished me happiness in our marriage."

"Which you denied."

"Of course, but in such a way she didn't believe me. I wonder why."

"Because she's also embarrassed by her daughter's running off. And I think she believed your heart might be involved. So she would be relieved if you were involved with someone else. No matter how unsuitable."

"You are not unsuitable," he replied.

Bethanne didn't respond. He still thought her the daughter of a thief. She was tired and wanted to go to bed. Tomorrow they'd return to Quishari and the goodbyes that waited.

"You are a kind man, Rashid. It was good of you to save face for them. It will make the working relations run more smoothly in the future."

The next morning they took off early, leaving Marrakech just awakening in the dawn. Once again the plane was refueled in Cairo. Then began the final leg of the trip. It was growing dark as they flew over the Quishari western border. Before long scattered lights speckled the landscape below them. The skies were full of stars, so much clearer at this elevation. Bethanne loved flying at night. There was something special about rocketing through the darkness with only the stars as a guide.

She checked her coordinates and contemplated her next move. If Rashid wasn't going to help, she'd have to do it herself.

Rashid rested his head on the sofa cushions. He was tired. The dealing with his new associate had been long and more difficult because of Haile's actions. To pretend things were fine when they weren't went against his grain. He was all for openness and honesty—where it didn't hurt anyone. Having Bethanne along, pretending he was involved with her, had given his host a way to save face. The deal was too important to end up contentious because of a willful woman's actions. But the strain of being with her and yet not wore on him.

The airplane shifted slightly. Rashid opened his eyes. Glancing at his watch, he saw it was too early to be landing in Alkaahdar. Yet it definitely felt as if the plane was descending. Was there a problem?

He rose and walked to the cockpit just as Bethanne spoke into the microphone, "Fasten up."

"Is there a problem?" he asked.

She shook her head, concentrating on the task at hand. "You need to sit down and fasten your seat belt," she said.

"Why are we descending?"

"We're landing."

He slipped into the copilot's seat and looked out. The blackness below went on for miles, with only a speck of light here and there and a small glow in front of them. Ahead was an array of lights—a runway.

"Where are we?"

"Buckle up, Rashid. We're going to land in about five minutes and if it's bumpy, you don't want to be tossed around."

He snapped on the belt and reached out to take her arm.

"Where are we?"

"Airborne over Quishari, soon landing in Quraim Wadi Samil."

"No."

"Oh, yes," she said softly.

He heard the determination in her tone. Unless he knew how to take control of the plane, there was nothing he could do.

"I'll call your office and have you fired."

"Go for it." She flicked him a glance. "I came to Quishari with two purposes. To deliver the plane and to find my father. I'm not going home when I'm so close. Now, I would like to concentrate on the landing, so kindly keep quiet."

Rashid was struck by the novelty of having someone telling him to shut up. Did she know who he was?

Of course she did, and was not a bit intimidated by the fact. She claimed to love him. Yet she had not repeated that statement once he'd shown her he couldn't be persuaded. Had it been a gambit?

With a resignation that the truth was probably she had tried that to get his cooperation, he settled back and watched her bring the jet in with a perfect landing.

It was not so late the airport wasn't still functioning. But late enough they were probably the last plane to land this evening. Quraim Wadi Samil didn't qualify as a hot spot in the world of travel.

She taxied where directed and shut down the engines.

"We're here," she said.

"Do you plan to go to the cemetery in the dark?"

She shook her head. "I plan to find a room somewhere, sleep until morning and then go. After you get the location from your assistant. If you want me to, I'll take you to Alkaahdar before leaving for Texas."

"And if I call your home office to have you dismissed?"

"As I said, go for it. I may never get this chance again. I need to know for absolute certain." She rose and went to get her small suitcase and open the door. Walking down the steps, she turned toward the terminal.

Rashid was tempted to call her bluff. She had openly defied him. He sat down in the seat and considered his options.

He knew why she had landed here. If it had been his father, wouldn't he do all he could to find out the truth? To learn what happened?

He reached in his pocket for the cell phone and called his assistant at home. It was late, but he needed answers now.

Rashid checked into the hotel they'd used when last in

Quraim Wadi Samil. He verified Bethanne was already there before heading up to his room. He had a lot of thinking to do.

The next morning, he waited in the lobby until she came down. Crossing to her, he took her arm and pulled her aside.

"I've ordered a car to take us to the cemetery near the older part of town. I know where your father is buried."

She looked at him in astonishment. "You're kidding. Have you always known?"

"I learned of it last night. Come, we have time before the car comes to have breakfast. Have you eaten?"

She shook her head.

They sat in the sunshine in the small courtyard off the main restaurant adjacent to the hotel. Once their orders had been given and the waiter left, Rashid began.

"I called my assistant last night. He had talked with Hasid. Then I called Khalid."

"Khalid?" Bethanne said, puzzled.

"He is the sheikh Hasid spoke with, not me."

Of course, both the twins were sheikhs. Hasid had nodded toward where Rashid and Khalid had been speaking. In his mind he probably thought she knew who he meant.

"And?"

Rashid looked around, as if assuring himself they would not be overheard.

"I owe you an apology, Bethanne. Your father's friend was correct. Hank was doing a special favor for my father—a secret assignment, as said. He came here to Quraim Wadi Samil to pick up someone special. The flight was cut short with a freak sandstorm shortly after they departed the airport. They were blown off course, or flew wide trying to avoid the sand. But the plane crashed. Everyone on board died."

Bethanne stared at him. Rashid tried to gauge her feelings, but her expression was wooden. "What was the secret?"

He didn't want to tell her. He didn't want to believe it, but his brother had made it clear it was the truth. After accusing her father—he owed her the truth.

"A daughter my father had with a woman not his wife. He wanted to see her before sending her to finishing school in Switzerland. Hearing of her death triggered his heart attack and he died. Khalid has known, and chose not to reveal it to anyone. Until I forced it out of him last night."

She still didn't say anything.

"My apologies for accusing your father. Had I known the truth from the beginning, I would never have said such a thing."

"So you know where he's buried?" she asked.

"I have directions."

She nodded and then stared around the courtyard as if she didn't know where she was.

"I'm sorry, Bethanne."

She nodded again. "Does your mother know?" she asked.

"No. Khalid's rationale was no one needed to know. He never expected Hank's daughter to show up. When I told him who you were, he finally agreed to tell me everything. He was protecting my mother."

"And you," she said slowly.

He nodded. "It's hard to discover the honorable man I revered my entire life had cheated on his wife and had another child. One, moreover, he spent a great deal of time with. I thought his reasons for keeping the oil fields operational and under such close observation was he wanted the best for the people of Quraim Wadi Samil. Turns out it was a cover for visiting his mistress and child."

"Now I'm the one who's sorry. That has to be hard to learn at this late date."

"I can deal with it. It's my mother who continues to need protecting. Fortunately he was circumspect and few people knew of the situation. Now that the daughter is dead, and my father, the story is unlikely to come out."

The waiter reappeared with their breakfast. Conversation ended while they ate. Rashid wished Bethanne would say something. But he couldn't have said what. She had a lot to forgive with his family. If he'd told Khalid sooner, would he have told Bethanne the truth immediately? Before he had a chance to know her, to grow to care for her?

After they finished eating, they summoned a hired car. Rashid gave directions to the cemetery and when they reached it instructed the driver to wait. The graveyard was dusty and brown. Few scraggly plants grew, no grass. The tombstones were lined up in rows. The main path cut the grounds in half.

Bethanne looked at the tombstones as they walked through one section. Her heart was heavy. Tears threatened. She had known for a long time her dad was dead. He would not have ignored her this long had he not been. But she had clung to hope as long as she didn't know for sure. Now that hope was gone.

As if he knew exactly where he was going, Rashid led her across a series of sections and stopped in front of a newer stone. Hank's name was in English. Other words were carved in Arabic. She hadn't a clue what they said.

"What does the inscription say?" she asked, staring at the foreign script.

"It says, 'Here rests a true friend, loyal to the end.'"

"Probably not the words that would be used if he were a thief," she murmured. She wished the words had been in English.

"Hi, Dad. I found you," she said softly. She knelt on the ground, reached out and touched the stone. It was already warm from the sun. Memories flashed through her mind. She loved her father. Felt curiously happy to find him, even though he had died three years ago. She had known it all along, just denied it. He would not have ignored her for so long had he been on earth. The cards and letters had came sporadically, but the phone calls had been as regular as the sunrise.

She wouldn't have been a pilot if he hadn't fostered the love of flying in her. She wouldn't have seen as much of the world as she had. And he wouldn't be lying here now at age fifty-two if he hadn't been who he was. Wild and free, only touching down when he had to. Otherwise the skies were his home.

Would she end up like he had? Alone, far from her native land? Having lived life the way she wanted?

She glanced at Rashid. One thing she wanted she wasn't going to get.

"How did you know right where he was buried?" she asked.

Rashid was silent for a moment, staring at the headstone. "Khalid told me. And where our half sister lies. I want to see that stone as well. I didn't know I had a sister until last night."

"The mechanics at the airport said Hank stole the plane and vanished. That the sheikh's son didn't know anything. Hasid said he'd told you."

"No. I didn't know. But Khalid did. He was the one who discovered what happened when they didn't arrive as planned. She was to go to college in Europe and my father wanted to see her before she left."

"How was he planning to do that without your mother's knowledge?"

"I have no idea. But she doesn't know. She would be so hurt. She herself always wanted a daughter."

Bethanne looked at the graves marching away from her father.

"And where is her place?"

"Come, Khalid told me. It was he who arranged the stones.

He who took care of everything, careful to keep our father's name out of it."

Bethanne rose and touched the stone again. She would in all likelihood never be here again. She'd found her father, only to have to say softly, "Goodbye, Dad."

Rashid led the way down several rows. Soon they stood before a stone engraved completely in Arabic.

"The place next to it is saved for her mother. She loved my father and he loved her. When they met—when he came to start the oil fields—he was already married with two sons. According to Khalid, the arranged marriage with my mother was important in a business sense. Yet he wanted to end it. My mother would not without causing a scandal and pulling out the money that would have sunk the business back then. In the end he stayed married to her. He told Khalid this as he was dying. He visited Quraim Wadi Samil as often as he could, enjoying his daughter and spending time with the woman he loved. He swore to Khalid our mother never knew.

"The plane crash and his daughter's death caused his own heart attack and death. Khalid never made the facts known. It would do nothing for those who died. He said he'd rather have the living content with life as they knew it. What point to shatter that?"

"I'm so sorry, Rashid," she said simply. She had no idea of the circumstances. Yet she was glad he had not known and not told her. She was glad her father had been helping someone when he died. It sounded more like him than being a thief.

"You once said truth always comes out. This is one I hope doesn't," he said.

"I understand. Thank you for telling me. And restoring my faith in my father. I never believed what you thought."

"Ironic, isn't it?" he said.

"What?"

"Hank was a loyal employee of our company and a loyal friend to my father. A man trusted to carry his most precious daughter. A man of integrity. It was a tragedy to end as it did."

She looked around the cemetery, imprinting it on her mind. She'd remember the words on the stone. Remember he'd died trying to help a friend.

"Instead, it was my father who was less than honorable. I'm sorry, Bethanne, for doubting your father."

"I'm ready to leave now," she said, turning away lest he see the tears in her eyes. She'd never hug her robust father again. Never get a card or letter. Never be able to tell him how much he'd meant to her—even though they rarely saw each other. She knew he'd known, but the plans they'd made—for some-day—would be carried out solo now. She had his memory and his love of flying. It would have to be enough.

"Thank you for bringing me. I will honor the secret. I would do nothing to hurt your mother," she said as they walked slowly back through the cemetery.

"Her behavior could be better toward you."

"She doesn't like me. That's okay. She doesn't need to." Bethanne stopped at the gate, the hired car only a few yards away.

"Truth always comes out. I'm glad you found out before I left. And told me. If I hadn't been able to wrangle the flight to deliver the plane, I would never have gotten to know you, and that would have been my loss. I'm grateful for all you've done for me. I wish you the best life has to offer, Rashid."

He studied her for a moment. This was the time for him to say something, if there was anything to say. He merely in-clined his head.

"And you, Bethanne."

Bethanne summoned a smile and turned, walking swiftly to the car. There was nothing left to say.

* * *

When the jet landed in Alkaahdar, she finalized all the details for leaving the plane near the private hangar. Taking her bag, she saw Rashid had already disembarked. She carefully withdrew the beautiful dress from her case, along with the shoes and golden necklace. Putting them on the sofa, she was sure they wouldn't be overlooked. Glancing around once more, she smiled. This jet was the best Starcraft had to offer. She knew Rashid would get years of service from it. She'd think about him from time to time, imagining him flying high in the plane. And she'd remember the times they'd flown together.

"Bless this aircraft and all who fly it," she murmured before leaving.

When she reached the tarmac, she looked around for a conveyance to take her to the main terminal. She had a flight to Texas to catch.

CHAPTER NINE

"So THE deal is signed," Khalid said.

"It is. We begin to implement next week," Rashid returned. He looked up from his desk. "What are you doing here?"

"Came to say goodbye for a while. I'm heading inland on another consultation job for a new field opening up. I'll be gone a few weeks, probably."

"The Hari fields?"

Khalid nodded, walking around the office. He touched one of the statues on the bookcase, then went to the window.

"Where's your pilot?"

"She's not my pilot."

Khalid turned at that. "You could have fooled me. You seemed as besotted with her as you were with Marguerite."

"Then that should have told you something."

"Only I don't think Miss Bethanne Sanders is anything like Marguerite."

"Don't bet the oil field on it," Rashid said.

Khalid raised an eyebrow in silent question.

Rashid hesitated, but Khalid was his twin.

"She wanted something from me after all."

"Money?"

He shrugged. Hesitating a moment, he looked up. "She said she loved me. Once."

Khalid stopped and stared at his twin.

"And that's a problem because?"

"She was trying to get info on Hank."

"That must have hit her hard, when she learned you thought he'd stolen the plane."

Sighing at the inevitability, Rashid related the entire story to his brother.

"I wanted you to remember our father with love. How honorable was it for him to have another family?" Khalid said. "I never expected anyone from Hank's family to show up. Was she hurt when she discovered his death?"

He shook his head. "I believe she'd known all along, just kept hoping. I'm the one in the wrong, accusing her father of theft when it was ours who acted dishonorably. Did you ever meet her? Our sister? What was she like?"

"I didn't know about her until after her death," Khalid said. "Father had pictures of her. He loved her mother and her. I have the photos. You can look at them if you wish."

"So there is love in the world," Rashid said.

"Which doesn't always bring happiness. Do you think any of them were happy?"

"Maybe the daughter, cherished by both her parents."

"At least he went after the love he wanted. Ever think you should have gone after Marguerite?"

Rashid shook his head. "But I'm thinking of going after Bethanne."

"Why not?" Khalid asked.

"You're suggesting that I should? I thought you didn't like her."

"I like her fine. I was worried she was after something else. But if she wanted closure about her father, that's different."

"She doesn't care about me—she only wanted to find out about her father."

"There were other ways to do that than pretend to be involved with you. To say she was in love."

"You thought she was after something and she was."

"Family. Not money. There's a big difference," Khalid said.

Rashid nodded. "She wished me a good life." He remembered how he'd fought to resist taking her into his arms when she'd said that. He had let her go without telling her he wanted her more than anything—even his next breath.

"She's gone?"

Rashid shook his head. "I still haven't signed off on the new jet. She can't leave before then. That's as important to her as finding her father was."

"Then I suggest you decide if you want to end up like our father, or maybe grab for the gold ring first time round," Khalid said.

Rashid drove to the villa as soon as Khalid left. Entering, he called for Bethanne. Minnah came into the foyer.

"Excellency, she is not here. She took you to Morocco. Did she not fly you back?"

"She did, earlier this morning. She didn't return here?"

"No. I have not seen her."

He turned and went back to the car. Where would she be? He never knew what to expect with her. Was she still at the plane like in Marrakech? Rashid headed for the airport, feeling a sense of déjà vu.

A quick cursory inspection upon arrival showed the jet empty—except for the dress he'd bought her in Marrakech. She truly had wanted nothing from him except to find her father. A woman more unlike Marguerite he'd never find.

He pulled out his cell phone and called his office, setting every assistant he had with the task of finding Bethanne Sanders. He also instructed them to let him know the minute the Starcraft office opened in Texas. He had to find her and he was calling in all markers to do so.

Impatiently Rashid drove back to his office. He would find out more from there than running around town. Walking in, he began to fire questions at his assistant.

"Did you check the local hotels? How about car rental companies? Car hire companies. She has to be somewhere."

The assistant nodded. "We've been checking every place in the capital city, Excellency."

"I have a confirmation," one of the clerks said, looking worried.

"And?" Rashid snapped.

"She departed the airport at eleven on a flight to Rome."

Rashid couldn't believe she'd left.

He went into his office and closed the door.

Bethanne watched as the smoggy air of Rome seemed to encase the airliner as it descended into Leonardo Da Vinci Airport. She had several hours to wait for a connecting flight to New York. Time enough to visit a few of the highlights of the city. She couldn't muster much enthusiasm for that, however. Still, who knew if she'd ever be in Rome again? And it beat the other choice—sit and brood.

When they landed, she waited until more impatient passengers had deplaned, then followed. Finding a locker, she stowed her flight bag and went to find a cab to drive her around the city. Her flight did not depart until ten that evening. She had time to see some of Rome and get a fabulous dinner before heading for the United States.

Despite her best efforts, Bethanne couldn't help comparing what she saw in the city with the buildings and architecture she'd loved in Quishari. Both countries were old, both rich in history. She was fascinated by all she saw and wished she could share it with Rashid.

How long would it be until she no longer felt his loss like a part of her had been cut out? She knew she would survive, but wasn't sure she wanted to. She *ached* with longing to see him again. Touch him. Share a warm kiss. Go sailing or flying. Or just spend the evening on the veranda listening to the waves of the sea.

Hours later, after finishing her dinner, she took another taxi back to the airport. The city gleamed with lights, looking beautiful in the soft illumination. But Bethanne was blind to it all. It was all she could do to keep from bursting into tears.

She probably had no job. Would be hard-pressed to find another one as perfect as this one had been. She had walked away from the only man she'd ever loved, which had been the hardest thing she'd ever done. Harder than acknowledging finally that her beloved father was gone. Raw emotions had her so confused. She wanted to go home, crawl into bed and weep for a week.

Her future was uncertain, except for the ache in her heart. She pressed a hand against her chest, trying to ease the pain.

She'd found her father, but would have traded that for another few days with Rashid al Harum. Pretending they were falling in love.

Or not pretending, falling for real.

She retrieved her flight bag when she reached the airport. Shopping at one of the kiosks there, she couldn't find any books in English. She'd do better to sleep on the flight, but was too keyed up. Finding a couple of magazines she could look at, she headed for her gate.

"Bethanne."

Turning, she stared at Sheikh Rashid al Harum. Or a man

who looked a lot like him. She shut her eyes tightly, then opened them. He still stood in front of her.

"Rashid?" she asked tentatively.

"You constantly surprise me. Makes for an interesting relationship."

"What are you doing here?"

"I'm flying to the United States on a flight that leaves at ten. You?"

She licked her lips. "I'm leaving on that flight, too. Why are you going to the United States?"

"To spend time with you, of course."

"Of course? There's no of course. You made your feelings perfectly well known to me."

"Perhaps we have a minor misunderstanding."

"Rashid, what's going on?"

"I didn't expect you to leave like that. I guess I expected more Yankee tenacity."

"What are you talking about? You practically ordered me to leave. I don't understand."

He glanced at his watch, stepped out of the way of a porter with a trolley of bags. Taking her arm, he pulled her to the side of the concourse. "It's not often I admit to making mistakes. I try not to make them to begin with. But I made a monumental one with you."

"Pretending to be involved?" That hurt.

"Not admitting when the pretense ended."

"When you signed the contract in Marrakech," she said.

"No, when it changed to love."

Bethanne's eyes widened. "If you're throwing that up to me—"

"What I'm trying to say is that I love you."

Rashid smiled at her look of astonishment, dropping his brief-case and pulling her into his embrace, kissing her on the mouth.

"Rashid!" she exclaimed when she pulled back. "This is a public place."

"So? I want the world to know I love you. What better place to start than here?"

"Here?"

"Everyone is greeting someone or bidding them farewell. Kisses are not out of the ordinary. Though I prefer our kisses to be in private. I don't wish to share."

"Did you say you loved me?" she asked.

"I did. I'll say it again. I love you, Bethanne Sanders. I fought against it. I didn't want to fall in love—my experience with that emotion has not been good. But foolish thought, that I can control emotions. You are all I have ever sought for in a partner. Beautiful, smart, talented in ways I can't compete, and interesting enough to keep me enthralled for decades."

She laughed, throwing her arms around his neck. "I am so unsuitable to be the wife of Arabian royalty. I'm much too casual in dress and manner to impress your associates. I want to fly whenever I can and I really don't think your mother is going to be at all happy with this. But I love you! I've been in the biggest funk ever since I left Alkaahdar. I thought I'd never see you again."

"I couldn't believe you left." He hugged her tightly, as if he'd never let her go. "So does this mean you will marry me? Live with me in Quishari? Spend our nights together, maybe even have a few kids to round things out? I love you, my dearest Bethanne. Will you marry me?"

She stared at him, faces so close she could not see anything around them. Her heart pounded. He'd asked her to marry him. Dare she risk it?

Dare she refuse?

"I would be so honored, but you must know what you're doing first."

"Oh, I know exactly what our life will be like. We'll live at the villa. My grandmother loved that house. We can raise our children to love the sea and the air. Will you insist on their learning to fly?"

"Perhaps not insist. But if they love it, we can't stand in their way. Are you serious? About everything? Marriage, children? You and me?"

"I love you. Why wouldn't I want to spend the rest of my life with you? I thought a lot about my father and his love and daughter in Quraim Wadi Samil. His happiness could not be complete because he never severed the legal bonds that kept him from staying with the woman he loved. I don't want to be dying and regret a single moment we spent apart."

"I never thought I'd get married. I wanted the life my father had—flying around the world. But he found his spot in Quishari. He lived there the longest of any place after he was an adult. And I know why. I love what I've discovered about Quishari. I think I would be happy living there. And flying wherever the mood takes us."

"I have just the plane for that."

The announcement for their flight was made.

He hugged her and then released her. "So, do we go on to the U.S. or back to Quishari?"

"Whichever you choose," she said.

"Ah, the perfect answer for a perfect wife-to-be." He dropped a quick kiss on her lips.

"This time. I'm not planning to become a yes person," she warned, warmth in her voice.

He laughed, clasping her hand in his and retrieving his briefcase. "I never expected that. I'll take it when I can get it. Let's go to Texas so I can meet your parents and tell them of our plans."

"My mother is going to be astonished." And, she bet her

mother would be thrilled to know her daughter was marrying a sheikh.

"I believe my mother will be as well," he said wryly.

"I told you, I value truth. Your mother's honest. Maybe she'll come around one day, or maybe not. It will never change how I feel about you. I love you. I always will."

"That I'll hold you to." He lifted her hand to kiss it. "I will always love you," he vowed. "Come what may, we'll always have to look for clear skies and smooth flights."

"Always."

The future beckoned bright with happy promise.

* * * * *

Harlequin offers a romance for every mood!
See below for a sneak peek
from our paranormal romance line,
Silhouette® Nocturne™.
Enjoy a preview of REUNION by USA TODAY bestselling
author Lindsay McKenna.

Aella closed her eyes and sensed a distinct shift, like movement from the world around her to the unseen world.

She opened her eyes. And had a slight shock at the man standing ten feet away. He wasn't just any man. Her heart leaped and pounded. He reminded her of a fierce warrior from an ancient civilization. Incan? She wasn't sure but she felt his deep power and masculinity.

I'm Aella. Are you the guardian of this sacred site? she asked, hoping her telepathy was strong.

Fox's entire body soared with joy. Fox struggled to put his personal pleasure aside.

Greetings, Aella. I'm the assistant guardian to this sacred area. You may call me Fox. How can I be of service to you, Aella? he asked.

I'm searching for a green sphere. A legend says that the Emperor Pachacuti had seven emerald spheres created for the Emerald Key necklace. He had seven of his priestesses and priests travel the world to hide these spheres from evil forces. It is said that when all seven spheres are found, restrung and worn, that Light will return to the Earth. The fourth sphere is here, at your sacred site. Are you aware of it? Aella held her breath. She loved looking at him, especially his sensual mouth. The desire to kiss him came out of nowhere.

Fox was stunned by the request. *I know of the Emerald Key*

necklace because I served the emperor at the time it was created. However, I did not realize that one of the spheres is here.

Aella felt sad. Why? Every time she looked at Fox, her heart felt as if it would tear out of her chest. *May I stay in touch with you as I work with this site?* she asked.

Of course. Fox wanted nothing more than to be here with her. To absorb her ephemeral beauty and hear her speak once more.

Aella's spirit lifted. What *was* this strange connection between them? Her curiosity was strong, but she had more pressing matters. In the next few days, Aella knew her life would change forever. How, she had no idea....

Look for REUNION
by USA TODAY bestselling author Lindsay McKenna,
available April 2010, only from Silhouette® Nocturne™.

ROMANCE, RIVALRY AND A FAMILY REUNITED

THE BRIDES of BELLA ROSA

William Valentine and his beloved wife, Lucia, live
a beautiful life together, but when his former love Rosa
and the secret family they had together resurface,
an instant rivalry is formed. Can these families
get through the past and come together as one?

Step into the world of Bella Rosa
beginning this April with

Beauty and the Reclusive Prince
by
RAYE MORGAN

Eight volumes to collect and treasure!

www.eHarlequin.com

HR17650

OLIVIA GATES

BILLIONAIRE, M.D.

Dr. Rodrigo Valderrama has it all…
everything but the woman he's secretly
desired and despised. A woman forbidden
to him—his brother's widow.
And she's pregnant.

Cybele was injured in a plane crash
and lost her memory. All she knows is
she's falling for the doctor who has swept her
away to his estate to heal. If only the secrets
in his eyes didn't promise to tear
them forever apart.

Available March wherever you buy books.

Always Powerful, Passionate and Provocative.

Visit Silhouette Books at www.eHarlequin.com

SD73018

HARLEQUIN®

INTRIGUE

WILL THIS REUNITED FAMILY
BE STRONG ENOUGH TO EXPOSE
A LURKING KILLER?

FIND OUT IN THIS ALL-NEW
THRILLING TRILOGY FROM TOP
HARLEQUIN INTRIGUE AUTHOR

B.J. DANIELS

WHITEHORSE
MONTANA

Winchester Ranch

GUN-SHY BRIDE—*April 2010*

HITCHED—*May 2010*

TWELVE-GAUGE GUARDIAN—
June 2010

HI69465

LARGER-PRINT BOOKS!

GET 2 FREE LARGER-PRINT NOVELS PLUS
2 FREE GIFTS!

HARLEQUIN®

Romance

From the Heart, For the Heart

YES! Please send me 2 FREE LARGER-PRINT Harlequin® Romance novels and my 2 FREE gifts (gifts are worth about $10). After receiving them, if I don't wish to receive any more books, I can return the shipping statement marked "cancel." If I don't cancel, I will receive 6 brand-new novels every month and be billed just $4.34 per book in the U.S. or $4.99 per book in Canada. That's a saving of almost 17% off the cover price! It's quite a bargain! Shipping and handling is just 50¢ per book in the U.S. and 75¢ per book in Canada.* I understand that accepting the 2 free books and gifts places me under no obligation to buy anything. I can always return a shipment and cancel at any time. Even if I never buy another book from Harlequin, the two free books and gifts are mine to keep forever.

186 HDN E4HN 386 HDN E4HY

Name	(PLEASE PRINT)

Address	Apt. #

City	State/Prov.	Zip/Postal Code

Signature (if under 18, a parent or guardian must sign)

Mail to the Harlequin Reader Service:
IN U.S.A.: P.O. Box 1867, Buffalo, NY 14240-1867
IN CANADA: P.O. Box 609, Fort Erie, Ontario L2A 5X3

Not valid for current subscribers to Harlequin Romance Larger-Print books.

Are you a current subscriber to Harlequin Romance books and want to receive the larger-print edition? Call 1-800-873-8635 today!

* Terms and prices subject to change without notice. Prices do not include applicable taxes. N.Y. residents add applicable sales tax. Canadian residents will be charged applicable provincial taxes and GST. Offer not valid in Quebec. This offer is limited to one order per household. All orders subject to approval. Credit or debit balances in a customer's account(s) may be offset by any other outstanding balance owed by or to the customer. Please allow 4 to 6 weeks for delivery. Offer available while quantities last.

Your Privacy: Harlequin Books is committed to protecting your privacy. Our Privacy Policy is available online at www.eHarlequin.com or upon request from the Reader Service. From time to time we make our lists of customers available to reputable third parties who may have a product or service of interest to you. If you would prefer we not share your name and address, please check here. ☐

Help us get it right—We strive for accurate, respectful and relevant communications. To clarify or modify your communication preferences, visit us at www.ReaderService.com/consumerchoice.

HRLP10

▼ *Silhouette*®

SPECIAL EDITION

**INTRODUCING A BRAND-NEW MINISERIES
FROM *USA TODAY* BESTSELLING AUTHOR**

KASEY MICHAELS

SECOND-CHANCE
BRIDAL

At twenty-eight, widowed single mother
Elizabeth Carstairs thinks she's left love behind
forever....until she meets Will Hollingsbrook.
Her sons' new baseball coach is the handsomest
man she's ever seen—and the more time they
spend together, the more undeniable the
connection between them. But can Elizabeth
leave the past behind and open her heart to
a second chance at love?

FIND OUT IN

SUDDENLY A BRIDE

*Available in April
wherever books are sold.*

HARLEQUIN Romance®

Coming Next Month

Available April 13, 2010

HRCNMBPA0310